A032842732

KU-663-493

NURSE SALLY'S LAST CHANCE

Perhaps it wasn't always her fault, but somehow Sally Marsdon seemed to attract trouble wherever she went. She had been in continuous hot water for a long time – and now, in desperation, her family and friends – headed by the interfering family doctor, Bruce Carmichael – had decided to give her one last chance to settle down, and persuaded her to take up nursing. Sally was convinced that if only Dr Carmichael would mind his own business things would sort themselves out – but Dr Carmichael seemed determined to keep an eye on her...

NURSE SALLY'S LAST CHANCE

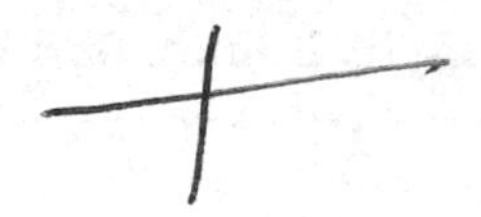

Nurse Sally's Last Chance

by

Anne Durham

CHESHIRE
LIBRARIES
0 9 AUG 2011
32208
MAG

Dales Large Print Books
Long Preston, North Yorkshire,
BD23 4ND, England.

British Library Cataloguing in Publication Data.

Durham, Anne
Nurse Sally's last chance.

A catalogue record of this book is
available from the British Library

ISBN 978-1-84262-838-6 pbk

First published in Great Britain 1967 by Mills & Boon Ltd.

Copyright © Anne Durham 1967

Cover illustration © Tony Meadow by arrangement with
Arcangel Images

The moral right of the author has been asserted

Published in Large Print 2011 by arrangement with
The Executor of Anne Durham,
care of S. Walker Literary Agency

All Rights reserved. No part of this publication may be reproduced, stored in a retrieval system, or transmitted in any form or by any means, electronic, mechanical, photocopying, recording or otherwise without the prior permission of the Copyright owner.

Dales Large Print is an imprint of Library Magna Books Ltd.

Printed and bound in Great Britain by
T.J. (International) Ltd., Cornwall, PL28 8RW

All the characters in this book have no existence outside the imagination of the Author, and have no relation whatsoever to anyone bearing the same name or names. They are not even distantly inspired by any individual known or unknown to the Author, and all the incidents are pure invention.

CHAPTER ONE

Sally Marston washed up at the kitchen sink with a vigour that wasn't really justified. She loathed washing up, but it was a job that kept the hands busy while one's thoughts roamed at will, their secret way. If you were doing something noisy and useful like washing up, she told herself grimly, the chances were that people would leave you alone. To be left alone was all that Sally asked for nowadays. Too much had been packed in that last year, things that she would have cheerfully mopped out like a child sponging a littered slate.

Behind her, in the big airy kitchen, Roberta was quietly ironing. Roberta bothered Sally. Roberta was about twenty-five, a sort of general factotum, ranging from part-time secretary to Sally's father, and part-time nurse to Sally's mother, but Roberta also acted as stand-in for the latest apology for a housekeeper, and at times Roberta drove the Marston car. Roberta was firmly ensconced in the family, to the extent of Sally's parents calling her Robbie, a thing Sally vaguely disliked. She herself had been away so long that home no longer seemed the same. Sally felt she herself was the outsider, Roberta the member of the family. But then, Sally had to admit fairly, Roberta's devotion to the family had earned her that place.

Roberta also had a smooth line of conversation, that began innocuously and then turned into something else, such as today an open invitation to confide in her. Sally suddenly hated Roberta and herself too, because confiding in someone was a thing she longed to do. Some people at nineteen were self-sufficient and didn't need to confide. Sally had regarded herself as one of these, and then she had realised that her world had started to crumble about her, and she couldn't think how it had happened, or indeed when it had even begun to do this.

Roberta said quietly, with that reasonable tone Sally's parents seemed to depend on, but which made Sally want to kick something, 'Your father isn't so well today.'

It was just a simple statement, but Sally read into it blame for David Marston's state of health, or even reproach for Sally not having noticed it.

'Did he say so?' Sally retorted.

'No. He'd never admit such a thing. I notice. I suppose it's because I'm here all day with both your parents. I watch them. He's been doing too much since your mother's accident.'

'Well, you can't blame me for that!' Sally was driven to say.

Roberta regarded her thoughtfully. 'You never asked exactly how it happened, did you? Your mother wonders why you never did.'

'I can't be sure anyone will tell me,' Sally said. The words were meant to be high-handed, but they sounded as though they were wrung from her. 'If you're determined to tell me, all right, I'm listening.'

'She was on the way to your school, to find out what was going wrong. She didn't want your father to worry, so she didn't ask him to drive her. She quietly went out and bought a rail ticket, but the express collided with a goods train.'

Sally shut her eyes for a minute. So that was how it had happened! That was the day she had slipped out to see Frank, only he hadn't been there, and it had rained. Her watch stopped when it fell off her wrist into a puddle and she missed the bus back and things went from bad to worse. That clot of a girl who shared her room had forgotten to open the window and Sally had been caught.

'I thought you might like to know about it,' Roberta went on. 'It might explain the stress between your parents. Your father didn't know why your mother was on that train and she wouldn't tell him, and I suppose he can't be blamed for wondering why she made a secret journey like that. He feels shut out.'

Sally felt ill inside. What was the underlying meaning there? she asked herself feverishly. Did Roberta know about her lovely mother's friendship with the man who had almost married her but finally lost her to Sally's father? Was that what Roberta was hinting at?

She stared down the length of the garden to where her parents were. Her mother was lying on the lounging chair. Never really able to walk again without a stick, marked for always by pain and suffering. Beyond the garden table sat Sally's father, and to her fevered imagination he seemed to be wilting under the heat of the sun's rays. Was it possible that he thought such a thing of her mother for making a journey without giving him the reason? Had Sally's mother kept her fears for Sally so well covered that her father hadn't suspected that all was not well with his own daughter, away at boarding school?

And did her parents blame her for her mother's accident? That was what mattered most.

'It was hardly my fault,' she found herself saying. 'And it really isn't any business of yours,' she couldn't resist adding.

'Actually it is,' Roberta said, still in that quiet voice. 'You see, both your parents have separately confided in me about it, but without betraying a confidence on either side, I can do nothing.'

Sally swung round. 'They *confided* in you?' Outrage was in her voice. To think they would tell this stranger, and not Sally herself! But then she had always seemed to be at arm's length from her parents.

Roberta watched her and read into that smooth, beautiful young face a dislike that wasn't altogether unexpected. She felt sorry for Sally.

The girl was such a young rebel, yet there was a lot of warmth in her, Roberta believed. David and his wife didn't understand such a complex character. They were lost as to how to deal with someone like their only daughter.

'A nurse gets confided in all the time, if

she loves her work,' Roberta said, with a faint smile.

'You're not a nurse!' Sally flared. 'Well, only part-time.' Roberta's practical manner and clean-scrubbed appearance, her good grooming achieved by much care and handicapped by a lack of any beauty at all, offended Sally. A person in Roberta's position shouldn't look like that. Like... Sally searched for words, and could only think of a person who was so firmly entrenched that she could afford to act as Roberta did.

'Actually I am a fully qualified nurse, but I do other things as well,' Roberta said diffidently.

'That's funny. In that case I should have thought you'd be earning more money elsewhere than we can afford to pay you. If you're so good at your job, why aren't you in hospital or something?'

'I happen to like private nursing better.'

You happen to like my father, Sally thought, but she kept her thoughts to herself now, forcing herself to turn back to the sink. She had never been so unhappy in her life, and that was saying something, after this last year. Frank Sandford, Quentin Farrell, and that job afterwards...

Across the sunlit garden a tall young man

strode, carrying a bag.

'Dr Carmichael!' Sally ejaculated, with distaste. 'What does *he* want? He practically lives in our house!'

'Well, he's come to see your mother, *and* your father, now hasn't he?' said Roberta, a question in her voice. 'You don't like him, do you? Why not? He's a very good doctor.'

'How can you know that, for certain?' Sally objected. 'All I can see is a man who is so good-looking it oozes out of his ears – and doesn't he know it! He's so pleased with himself, you can sense it, even from his back view!'

'I've seen his work,' Roberta said briefly. 'I was at the same hospital as he was.'

'You know everyone and everything, don't you? Hospital! Some potty little place, I suppose.' Sally was being bitter and childish and all the things she most disliked, but she couldn't stop herself. It was a choice of hitting out verbally or bursting into tears that would hurt and probably never cease.

'I wouldn't say the Princess Erlana's Hospital at Ventonbourne was a potty little place, but I suppose one is always prejudiced about one's own hospital,' Roberta remarked.

'Then why didn't he stay there, if it was so marvellous?' Sally cried, stung.

'He would have, so he told me once, only he had to come home and go into partnership with his father and when his father died, he had to keep on the practice.'

'Big deal!'

'What are *you* going to do with yourself, Sally, now the last job has finished?' Roberta asked quietly.

'What a delicate way of putting it! Don't you mean, now I've been fished out of yet another bowl of trouble? Trouble seems to be my middle name! Sally Trouble Marston, brought up with clinical care, educated in an expensive private school and sent to a simply too-too finishing school, and the only jobs I could get were – oh, never mind. I'm good for washing-up, aren't I? Look at that! Isn't that as your ladyship would wish it?'

Roberta said collectedly, 'Thank you, Sally. I'm grateful for any help. There's a lot to do, and I think there'll be more. I don't like your father's looks at all. Would you mind putting the ironing away for me? I want to go out and speak to Dr Carmichael.'

Sally watched her go, fury leaping through her. How near she had come to telling Roberta all about Frank, if only for the luxury of asking the final question: 'What do you think he went away for, like that, without a word to me?' made her shiver! She had nearly confided in Roberta, after all. Clever Roberta would surely have an answer to that question, all neatly worked out! But then nosey Roberta would know all about something Sally had never yet told anyone else.

Sally left the ironing where it was, and went to find her jacket. It was a lovely day and the woods and the lanes were beckoning. A walk might clear her head and allow her to think.

Dr Carmichael was crossing the hall, alone.

'Hello, Sally,' he said. To Sally's fevered imagination, the way he said it meant things like, 'you're a spoilt brat and I'd like to give you the punishment you deserve', or: 'what have nice people like your parents done to deserve a daughter like you?' Sally's back stiffened at the sight of him. Not that his very keen blue eyes were accusing so much as kindly, she saw, now she looked more closely at him. But kindness coming from him was not something Sally wanted.

To be honest, she didn't know why she felt such acute antagonism towards him. It was there, all the time, instinctively. She didn't like having to look up at him. His height made her feel inferior. She didn't like to feel that she was floating helplessly, not knowing where she was going or if anyone really cared, while here was a man who was sure where he was going, and was getting there under his own steam.

'Hello,' she said, in an unfriendly voice.

'Off somewhere?' he pursued.

'Naturally. I've done my stint for the day. I've washed up without Roberta having to ask me. I've made beds in the way Roberta says they should be done, hospital-fashion. I've scrubbed floors (well, one, anyway) because Mrs Brocklebank *says* her back won't let her today, and I've listened uncomplainingly to Roberta's life-story. Oh, yes, come to think of it, she must have been speaking the truth for once!'

'What does that mean?' he asked on a level note.

She shrugged. 'All that swank about being at a hospital, but I suppose it's true or she wouldn't have got all that housework routine to pass on to me. I suppose she was thrown out, too, because she was no good.'

'As a matter of fact, she was a very good nurse,' Dr Carmichael said, but he looked as if he were thinking of something else.

Sally said, watching him, 'I've just remembered! There's something I have to ask you, though I don't suppose you'll tell me. How did Roberta come to get this job here?'

Dr Carmichael took his time to answer. 'She was a nurse at the hospital where your mother was taken at the time of her accident, and she became attached to your mother.'

'But that's a year ago! And wait a minute – my mother went to Ventonbourne? What for? That's not on the way to my old school!'

'Did I say she went to Ventonbourne? Roberta was on loan to another hospital at the time – the one your mother was taken to. Why, Sally?'

'Oh, no reason. You wouldn't expect Mrs Marston's own daughter to want to know anything about her accident, would you?' she choked.

She rushed out before he could ask her any more questions, and he watched her thoughtfully. She ran with her head down, like a child. She was slender as a reed, with long shapely legs and pretty ankles. Her hair was the colour of pale toffee, or thick honey, and it shone, and swung about her. Heavy hair, clean, well brushed, expensively cut. Her eyes were stormy now, and darker than usual; a nice blue pair of eyes, deep-set, candid, quick to show hurt, and the speed with which she could be on the defensive. She reacted like someone who has been misjudged for too long, or not loved enough. And yet her parents doted on her…

She hadn't give him a chance to tell her what he had in mind to suggest to her, but then, he reminded himself ruefully, perhaps he hadn't made the right approach. It was difficult to know, with Sally, just what was the right approach.

She would have been very much surprised if she could have known the thoughts that were passing through Bruce Carmichael's mind just then. She had already decided that he didn't really like her. Her father, before the accident, had been very much interested in one special rose in his garden, but he had always put on very thick gloves before he went near it. That was how Bruce Carmichael made her feel, like that rose – a thing of beauty he had to put on gloves for, to get near; a thing too dangerous to trust.

Am I really like that?' she asked herself, as she swung down the lane into the paddock of Melchett's Farm. Here was her one friend: Ulysses, the neat little roan she used to ride. But Mick was out in the paddock and warned her to keep away.

'Turned nasty today, he did,' Mick explained laconically, as though it was no more than he expected of horseflesh. 'The boss said not to let you come near him. Expected you'd be over, he did.'

'Where is Mr Melchett now?' Sally asked, thinking it might be rather nice to have a chat with the elderly farmer who had once been a friend of her father's.

Mick avoided her eyes. 'He's right busy just now,' he said, and walked away.

Sally went hot and then quite icy. So that was how it was! Was this what they called the 'brush-off' on films? Had they heard that she was again home in disgrace? But surely the Melchetts didn't care about such things? They had laughed their heads off when their own boys had been sent home after some prank or other. But perhaps it was different in their eyes, in the case of a girl. The Melchetts were old-fashioned. She turned on her heel and walked out into the lane again. She liked animals, and got on well with them. A black and white terrier joined her and trotted by her side, looking up at her every now and then as if to give her silent sympathy. But even he abandoned her when he got to the village and saw a cat he liked to chase.

She must have stayed out a long time. The sun had gone in and a sharp little wind was frisking up, and she realised she was hungry.

She had walked six miles, and this was cross-country and no bus service to take her back home. She shrugged and set out to walk back.

Nearer home there was a field path for a short cut that would reduce the journey by a mile. Sally was conscious of sore feet. She hadn't changed her shoes. She was conscious, too, of the fact that this walk hadn't helped her, as it had in the past. She hadn't solved any of her problems. She had made a mess of everything and she couldn't see how it had been her fault. Each new attempt to start afresh seemed to land her in a bigger mess. Her parents didn't get any closer. It was becoming more and more difficult to know what to say to them. And there was Roberta, who never put a foot wrong, kept her place, yet had managed to earn the affection of both Sally's parents.

The field path came to an end by a ramshackle stile and a bank beyond it dropping sharply to the road. Without her usual caution at this point, Sally climbed the stile in preoccupied fashion, and slithered down to the bottom without looking. A car hurtled round the corner, screeched its brakes and stopped within yards of her, frantically sounding the horn.

Sally blinked, and looked into the indignant face of Dr Carmichael.

He got out and stood staring at her, too furious for the moment to say anything.

'You'll be killed if you go on like this!' he snorted at last. 'Well, get in – I was looking for you, anyway. Where have you been?'

She was about to refuse, but something in his manner stopped her. She got in and shut the door her side and waited. She was aware that her heart had started to quicken its beat uneasily, as if something were wrong at home. Why else should he have been looking for her?

'I went for a walk,' she said shortly. 'What did you want me for, doctor?'

'I was called back to your house again.' He glanced at her, and softened his voice a little. 'As a matter of fact, your father isn't so well.'

That was what Roberta had said! It was all Sally could do to restrain herself from saying it aloud and revealing her dislike of Roberta. She said instead, 'Yes, and what else?'

'Don't you care about your father, Sally?'

'Yes, I care,' she said fiercely. 'But all the caring in the world won't do a thing to ease the situation at home, and you know it. I can't get near to talk to him. He just looks pained and surprised, and my mother just keeps on saying that she can't understand me any more. If you're so full of ideas, why don't you find a solution to that one?'

'What went wrong, Sally?' he asked quietly.

The kindness in his voice was nearly her undoing. She couldn't have spoken if she'd wanted to, without breaking down. And she didn't want kindness from him.

'I think you must admit,' he continued, as the silence grew, 'that you were happy enough at that school of yours at first, and then things suddenly went wrong. If you could tell your parents, from the beginning–'

'Why were you looking for me?' she managed at last. 'Something's happened at home, hasn't it?'

He pulled into the side, and after the slightest hesitation, he said, 'Yes. Your mother had a fall.'

'A fall? How, for heaven's sake? I thought she could manage pretty well on those sticks? And where was Roberta?'

'Roberta had been on the point of going out to help your mother in from the garden, but the telephone rang. Your mother felt she might try to get in without help for once, but as she got to her feet, a dog streaked across the garden chasing a cat, and tripped her.'

'A dog?'

'Yes – a black and white terrier. I don't know who it belongs to, but the surprise element was as much to blame as the force the animal went against your mother's legs.'

The black and white terrier. A sharp intake of breath was the only sound Sally made, she was so shocked. It might well have been the terrier who had joined her for the first part of her walk. But there was no point in saying so. Dr Carmichael wouldn't have understood. His attitude was disgust for people who couldn't keep their animals at home.

She was aware he was sitting staring at her, waiting for some sort of answer, so she said, 'How badly was she hurt?'

'We don't know yet. Just shaken up, I would say. Roberta's looking after her until I can get a bed for her at the General.'

'Hospital?' Sally ejaculated. 'But–'

'The whole point is, the shock didn't do your father any good. He saw your mother go over, and he – well, he collapsed.'

She turned on him in a fury. 'Why didn't you tell me so at first? Where are they now? I must see my parents!'

'Take it easy. He'll be all right, with rest and care. I wanted to talk to you about that. I would like to send him – and your mother

– away for a bit, to a more gentle climate.'

'Have we got enough money for that? Have they agreed?' she asked blankly. There had always seemed to be enough money, until her mother's accident, but now she had the feeling that money was the most worrying thing in her father's life, and she could never reach him closely enough to ask. He just refused to discuss it with her.

'I believe there's a distant relative in France somewhere,' Dr Carmichael said. 'If they would consent to go there–'

'That won't help,' Sally said bluntly. 'There'd be rows. There always have been. The cousins don't like me.'

He said delicately, looking away, 'I was going to suggest that Roberta should be the one to go with them. She can give them the most help. There's a good man I know, in Switzerland, too, who might be able to do something for your mother, to help her to be more steady on her legs.'

Sally thought that over. 'What am *I* supposed to do?' she asked at length.

'Well, this has been under discussion for some days. I've talked to your parents about it by degrees, so that they shouldn't be worried. Having regard to what happened today, to make the thing more urgent, perhaps it's as well that I did talk it over with your parents.'

'Talk what over?' she stormed.

'Sally, what I'm trying to say is, they will be away for some time. There's the question of what will become of you, too, as you have no career.'

'So you've discussed my future with my parents, without referring to me! Fine, fine. And what about the house, if dear Roberta's going to France with Mummy and Daddy? Has anyone thought of that? Or am I supposed to keep it going?'

'The question of the house has been worrying them. They don't want such a big place, especially as your mother can't get upstairs.'

'So they're going to sell it? How, if they're going to be away in France, under treatment?' she gasped.

'Actually I have a patient who knows your house and would like to take it over. There shouldn't be any worry over it. Your parents' solicitors and my patient's lawyers will settle it all up between them. Your parents are very much relieved. They can do with the money.'

'Fine!' she said, after another long silence. 'So while I've been out walking, things have moved ahead quite a bit, and my parents gone and my home about to be shifted from under my feet. And what have you settled for me, Dr Fix-it-all?'

He smiled slightly, refusing to take umbrage. 'Now, Sally, be reasonable, my dear, and don't make an enemy of me. I'm doing my best for everyone. I've thought of something for you, though, with your record, bless me, it hasn't been easy.'

She whitened a little, but she refused to let him see how suddenly scared she was. 'Go on, tell me! I'm fascinated to know what you've cooked up for someone who can do nothing, but nothing, except ride a horse!'

'You've got intelligence, if you'll use it, to study. What other girls of your age can do, so can you. And didn't you tell me you had learned from Roberta how to wash up with a minimum of time wastage, and make beds the approved way?'

She stared at him, the awful truth dawning on her.

'Well, my dear,' he said, reasonably, 'it *is* a career, and it will offer you a roof over your head, and money while you're learning. There's a good social life, too, and you'll have friends, and your parents will have no more worries on your behalf. My old hospital–'

'Good grief, you can't mean it!' she gasped. 'You want me to become a nurse!'

CHAPTER TWO

It seemed to Sally that from that talk in Dr Carmichael's car, to the time when she presented herself at Princess Erlana's Hospital in Ventonbourne, she had been rushed forward with unseemly haste. Roberta and Bruce Carmichael between them had packed and despatched Sally's parents to the cousins, and before she had gone with them, Roberta had driven Sally to Ventonbourne for her interview with the Matron.

In the train to Ventonbourne, alone now, and starting yet another career, Sally remembered isolated things, snatches of conversation, odd looks from those close to her, and she tried to repress a shiver. What else had she expected? she asked herself. What else was likely to be done with her, after the hash she had made of everything so far?

She remembered her mother, in the local hospital, looking searchingly at her when Sally went to say goodbye.

'Wouldn't you like to tell me what started everything going wrong at that nice finishing school we found for you, dear?' her mother had said, in a hushed voice, almost as if she had been afraid to voice the question.

'What first made you think something was going wrong?' Sally asked, and that was a question she had wanted to ask for such a long time, too. But in this past year her mother's health had been a sufficient barrier to discussing anything of an irritating nature.

'Instinct, I suppose, and because you left so much unsaid in your letters. Underlying your letters was such an unhappy note,' her mother said reluctantly.

Sally experienced relief. 'Well, I was unhappy. Your money was being spent, and it wasn't getting us anywhere, but no one listens to me, so it was no good asking to leave,' she said.

'But the reason for your having to leave that school, my dear – who was the young man?'

Frank Sandford wasn't a young man. He was over thirty and sophisticated and hard and he had done practically everything already, including being married and left a widower. But Sally hadn't known that at first and it didn't seem the time to mention it now. So she said, 'Just a man-friend. No one of importance. The important thing was getting back after being locked out. No one forgave that, at that wonderful school.'

She and her mother had looked at each other then. Never had Sally wanted to confide in anyone more, but she couldn't, and she doubted if her mother would have believed what she had to say. Her mother would undoubtedly have been very upset. No, better left the way it was.

Sally sighed, and moved restively under the set gaze of the girl in front of her. She thought of her brief stay at the riding school, her first job, and of Quentin Farrell. Never again, Sally told herself, would she believe a man who said he loved her. It was such an easy thing to say, and in her experience no one ever really meant it.

She thought, with faint amazement, of the way her father had looked at her, when she had said goodbye to him.

'Your mother and I don't think very seriously about this last year, you know. We were distressed at first when you said you had to leave the riding school. It wasn't like you to be so hysterical about a job you didn't like. We did rather expect you to stay on, have a really good bash at it. After all, horses were your special interest, weren't they? But as I say, neither that nor the hotel receptionist job you threw up seriously worried us. What we would like to feel is that you might meet some nice young man and settle down, make a life of your own.'

He smiled deprecatingly as Sally's eyebrows shot up. 'I know it's an old-fashioned idea, Sally, but your mother and I tried it and we've been very happy together. There's such a lot you've missed, never knowing what it's like to share a life with a member of the other sex.'

Poor Daddy, what would he say if he had met Quentin Farrell, or even Antony Bosworth…? Again she shivered, and this time the girl facing her was moved to speak.

'I say, I can't help noticing that your labels say you're going to the Princess Erlana, too. So am I!'

Sally repressed the retort that sprang to her lips too often nowadays. A thing she had learnt from the derisive lips of the clerks in Antony Bosworth's office. *Big deal!* A silly, yet somehow crushing, pair of words, meaningless, yet carrying a load of bitterness, the way Sally uttered them. She said instead, 'How nice.'

'No, it isn't,' the girl said earnestly. 'I don't want to be a nurse!'

That quite unwittingly caught Sally's

attention, 'Neither do I! We really ought to shake on that! Why don't you want to be?'

The girl was plain, earnest, in every way a sharp contrast to Sally's golden good looks. Sally studied the rather white cheeks, the pale blue eyes behind the modern-shaped spectacle frames that were frankly overwhelming in that face, and the trembling, sensitive, yet quite nice-shaped mouth, innocent of lipstick. The girl's dark brown hair had had a good razor cut, but was too short, and the fringe didn't really suit her. She looked like a typist more than nurse, Sally thought.

'I've been in hospital as a patient, and I hated every minute of it. I can't stand hospitals!' the girl gasped.

'Then why go there? Much better to be honest and own up to that, at the start!' Sally told her.

'It would upset my family. They're all nurses or something to do with hospitals. My aunt is an Almoner.'

'What, in Ventonbourne?' Sally gasped.

'No, thank goodness. That's why I chose it. It's about the one hospital my family don't seem to have had any connection with. What about you?'

Sally shrugged. 'Home's folding up.

Nowhere for me to go, and I'm not good at anything. Besides, our dear doctor suggested it, and the parents approved heartily.'

'Then let's shake on it,' the girl said. 'My name's Oldham – Cerise Oldham.'

Sally winced. Never was there a less suitable name for anyone. She gave her name and they solemnly shook hands, then Cerise told Sally all about her life.

She wanted to be a business woman. She liked typing and figures, and dreamed of a life in a skyscraper office in London or New York. Nothing could have been further from the life she had had, with its talk of medicine and surgery, diseases and casualties, the Health Service and general practice. She yearned for the clack of commercial machines rather than the hiss of the steri-liser. She dreamed of travel with the boss, rather than pounding the wards on sore, tired, aching feet.

Sally felt warmed to her. Cerise had had no experience of men, it seemed, and her brilliance at school had been a handicap in her social life.

Sally said, 'You and I had really better team up. With your knowledge of hospital personnel and my knowledge of the social life, we should be able to help each other. Of course, in one way you might not care to team with me. I was no good at school and left under a cloud. I was caught out of bounds. And alas, I'm nineteen.'

'Well, so am I! Oh, that's *good!*' Cerise said fervently. 'To tell you the truth, I've been dreading being one year older than the other beginners.'

'What made you a late starter?' Sally asked suspiciously. 'Surely you haven't had a year of calamities, too? I don't believe in that sort of coincidence!'

'No,' Cerise admitted. 'I've had a year's commercial training. I bargained for it. I promised to go to be a nurse if they'd let me go to commercial school for twelve months first.'

'You're brighter than you look,' Sally said critically. 'I get it, and then you just blot your copybook so badly that at the end of twelve weeks they throw you out of what I believe is called the Preliminary Training School.'

'P.T.S.,' Cerise said automatically. She had heard all about that from the cradle upwards. 'No, I shall do my best. I shall qualify.' She said it with a calm certainty that staggered Sally. 'Well, why not? Why throw up a chance to learn something? I shall hate being on the wards, but who knows what value the studying part of it will be to me in the future?'

Sally sat back, silently. There had been a time when she had badly wanted to be a veterinary surgeon, but that was before she had left the riding school in such a hurry. As she had given her reason for that performance as a terror of tricky horses, a vet's career had been closed to her from then on.

It was raining when the train arrived. Cerise looked automatically for a bus, but Sally hailed a taxi. Cerise's luggage was utilitarian, practical, but Sally's was pale green leather, and there was twice as much as her new friend's.

'What did you bring, then?' Cerise asked, after she had watched the taxi driver load the green cases into the front of the cab, and her own brown case on the top.

'All the clothes I possess,' Sally shrugged. 'What else would I do with them? Home, my dear Cerise, is no more.'

'Actually you'll have to call me Oldham,' Cerise said diffidently. 'They use surnames in hospital. Did you know?'

'No, I didn't,' Sally said grimly, and mentally blamed Roberta for not briefing her. But then in all fairness, she remembered belatedly she hadn't given Roberta much chance. She had been so prickly to think that

Roberta and Dr Carmichael had fixed her future between them that she had avoided Roberta's company where possible.

'And we shall have to share bedrooms, I expect. Only the third-years and staff nurses get singles, usually.'

'Share? Oh, well, that's nothing in my life. At school it was luxury to have only one girl in your room with you. At my school, anyway. There were usually six to a room.'

Cerise digested that with respectful silence, and said nothing during the cab journey through the busy streets of Ventonbourne, but when they at last arrived at the hospital, she said suddenly: 'You know, of course, that P.T.S. is just as strict as a boarding-school, about out-of-bounds, and all that?'

Sally did no more than favour her with a cold look, for other things were on her mind. The taxi had gone in at the main gate and up a long, long drive and round the back of the hospital, to a large red-brick building which had a board outside announcing that it was the Princess Erlana's Nurses' Home, and during that long, long drive it had been borne home to Sally that she was now in a world of women. She saw far more women than men; nursing juniors, nursing seniors, ward sisters and women in long white coats.

Only one man in all that feminine coming and going, crossing lawns to buildings marked X-ray and Casualty, Orthopaedic Block and Children's Wing, and he was bent and elderly, and wore old-fashioned spectacles that kept falling off, to dangle helplessly on the end of an incredible black ribbon. She felt crushed. What had she done, in complying with the wishes of her parents, their nurse and their doctor?

Her spirits sank a little lower still when she saw the room she was to share with Cerise, and even lower when she met the other six new girls, in their 'set'.

It was a giggly world of school all over again, with Sister Tutor, bristling a little because this looked a most unpromising new batch, trying to implant in them a sense of calling, vocation, the seriousness of doing everything, even to the making up of the student nurse's cap.

There was a silly little frilly thing with fluffy fair hair and eyes that were too innocent to be believed, who was not surprisingly called 'Amanda', and a tall girl the others called Dinah, who was a Head Girl, if ever Sally had seen one. Dinah Howard was born to lead and to organise and Sally promised herself that she would keep out of that one's way. Just for three months, that was all it was. Twelve little weeks in this P.T.S. and by then surely Mummy and Daddy would be fit enough to come back to England or something would happen, so that she wouldn't have to stay imprisoned in this awful place with these girls.

Dinah looked down from her height and showed the others how to do the caps. She had caught on from the first moment. Amanda Pimm characteristically gave Dinah her cap to do for her. That would be the pattern, Sally thought. They'd all be doing Amanda's jobs if they weren't careful.

Dinah's friend was the inevitable vacuous type that Head Girl types seemed to collect – Norma Kershaw, she told Sister Tutor, and Sally thought, with a grim smile, that Sister Tutor was thinking Sally's own thoughts: there was a yes-girl if ever there was one.

Joan Underwood was sleepy-eyed, Spanish-looking, and when two medical students passed the windows, it wasn't difficult to see what interested Joan most in life. Gay Leatherdale made a joke of everything and thought the whole thing was going to be a riot of fun, but Mary Dane was serious, a little anxious, and quite clearly there to be a nurse and nothing else. Sally sympathised with Sister Tutor for a brief moment.

Her sympathy fled when she realised that she and Cerise would be living out their lives with the other six for those three months. Eating, sleeping, working, playing together – that was the pattern at the Princess Erlana's, just as rigid a pattern as the uniforms, the protocol, the time-tables.

'Didn't you know it was going to be like this?' Cerise asked curiously, when they at last went up to their shared room. 'Weren't you briefed at the interview?'

'No-o,' Sally admitted rather unwillingly. 'It's a bit different for me, in a way, I suppose. Matron would expect our doctor to tell me all that. It was quite a friendly interview, though I can't think why. I never thought she'd have me here – but there, she's his cousin.'

Cerise was abashed for a moment. Sally misunderstood. 'Well, you've got connection in your family, too,' she reminded Cerise.

'I know – that's why I came here. It isn't good to have connections. You'll wish you'd never had that connection with Matron before you're finished.'

'Not me! She might wish it, though, before we've done with each other!' Sally grinned. 'Well, I ask you! How does anyone think *this* is going to interest anybody? Look at this uniform! Purple, worn below the knees!'

'It isn't purple, it's lilac, and you can't expect to wear your skirts frightfully short, especially when we go on the men's wards,' Cerise objected quite seriously. 'What do you think of the rest of our set?'

'I think that before a week is out, Underwood will be kicked out for looking at the men with that melting sickening look, and Pimm will be sent home to her mother with six of the best. Leatherdale will be kicked out for larking and Kershaw sent home because she's too dim. If they can stand boysy types, I suppose Howard will get through, and of course dear Dane will make the grade.'

'And what about us?' Cerise said softly.

'I shall be kicked out on principle. I get thrown out wherever I go. Oh, you'll get through all right,' Sally finished generously. 'I really admire your determination, considering you were sickened at an early age. What were you a patient for, by the way?'

'Road accident,' Cerise said briefly.

'Oh! Sorry,' Sally said quickly.

'Don't misunderstand. I just had a broken leg, but it was what I saw going on all round me that put me off. The patient's eye view of other patients.'

Cerise unpacked quickly and neatly, then asked Sally if she should help her. Sally let her. A lifetime at boarding school had done nothing to teach her neatness or swiftness with packing and unpacking. The job had always bored her.

'Marston, you've got some lovely clothes,' Cerise said, without envy. 'Look at this gorgeous dance frock. I didn't bring one. I don't go to dances.'

Sally had tennis clothes and trim tailored pants and shorts, elegant suits and crisp summer dresses, and at least three handbags. 'I wonder if it's worth unpacking the lot,' she paused to say, thoughtfully.

She threw her slippers across the room, and one skidded under the chest. Cerise demurred. Sally's slippers were fur-edged and almost new. She bent to get it out and drew out a letter.

'This must have got blown underneath. I suppose it was stood up on the chest. It's for you Marston.'

Sally's hand shook as she took it. For an absurd fraction of time she thought it might be from Frank, sent from home. Ever since she had seen him last, she had waited for a letter from him. But this thick strong handwriting wasn't Frank's.

She slit it open, angry with herself for still getting upset over such a thing.

It was from Dr Carmichael. 'Dear Sally,' he wrote. 'Just a note to welcome you into your new life.'

She closed her eyes. What did he want to write to her for, raising her hopes like that? she thought angrily. He had persuaded her to come here to be a nurse. Why couldn't he leave her alone now?

There wasn't much more, so she read it to the end, and it fanned the flame of her anger again, although quite clearly he hadn't meant to.

'You may not like being in a world of women, and you will certainly chafe at the discipline, if I know anything about you. But there's always discipline, whatever you have to do or wherever you go, so make the most of it, my dear, and look on it as a chance to carve out a career for yourself. It wasn't easy to persuade my cousin to take you, even though she is Matron, because what you've done this last year was not really a recommendation, was it? I suppose you might say that this is your last chance of a career, because if you are requested to leave the hospital, even I won't be able to perjure my soul on your behalf.'

He sent every good wish and finished hers truly Bruce Carmichael. Sally screwed it into a ball and threw it into the waste paper basket, her face flushed with fury.

'Not a nice letter?' Cerise frowned. 'Pity. I was thinking how thoughtful it was of someone to welcome you in with a note like that. Rather a nice surprise, it could have been.'

'It could have been!' Sally echoed between her teeth. 'That was from our dear family doctor. Who does he think he is, to talk to me like that? Just because he's related to Matron! Honestly, he thinks – he expects – that I shall be thrown out! He says he's perjured his soul to get me here. What about that? I'll show him. My last chance, indeed!' She looked fiercely across the room at Cerise. 'He doesn't know me! I'm going to stay here and I'm going to qualify, just to show him! And you're going to help me, Oldham! All right, I've been expelled from school. All right, I left the riding school in an almighty hurry and I bet he'd like to know why! All right, he's drawn a discreet veil over what happened at my last job. But I'm sticking it out here! If it's the last thing I do, I'm sticking it out to the bitter end.'

CHAPTER THREE

Sister Tutor had her pet methods, and one of them was for the class to write a letter home reporting at the end of each week. Cerise wrote reams. It was expected of her. It would be passed round the family, to the two aunts who had been nurses, and her mother who had been a midwife; to the ward sister and the ex-Home Sister in the family, and of course the Almoner.

Sally cursed the system. She had never liked writing letters. Even to Frank, she hadn't managed to write love letters, though her heart had been bursting for him. She penned frustrated notes of short length, and was urged by Sister Tutor to write longer ones. Home Sister gave advice one night, on her rounds, to those who found letters home such a formidable task, to write them in diary form, a paragraph for every day. The staff nurse whose unenviable job it was to teach this batch to make perfect beds curtly said that it was no worse than writing lines at school, and from what she had seen of them, they had all had ample experience of that.

Sally wrote to her mother at the end of the first week that she had been reprimanded for her corners, (which gave her pleasure because Roberta would be told and Roberta was so pleased with her tuition of Sally over beds!) and that she had learned how to make bandages. There was also a skeleton they had to learn about bones.

She almost scratched that out, because if her mother was going to be operated on her legs, she probably wouldn't want to hear about her daughter's clumsy beginner attempts to name the joints. Sally thought she would feel rather uneasy about the nurses if she heard too much about their beginnings, but she didn't have a chance to alter her letter. Sister Tutor hustled them to pack them up for posting, before they changed their minds.

'Why don't you like writing letters to your mother?' Cerise asked her curiously, as they put their books away one day. It was the time when most of the new students heard each other recite their notes from the last lecture, and Sally had discovered that she could remember things if she actually did them with her hands, *saw* them. Written descriptions defeated her.

The bond between herself and Cerise grew daily, and without realising it, Sally was letting out little bits of information. 'My mother won't be the only one to read it,' she said curtly. 'There's her nurse.'

And that meant telling Cerise why Mrs Marston was in France, and about how Roberta had trained here.

'Roberta – what?' Cerise asked her.

'Roberta Nesbitt. Why?'

'Just wanted to know a bit more about her,' Cerise said thoughtfully. 'She's under your skin. Well, she *is* the person who helped you get ready to come here, isn't she? And you talked about that person as if you disliked her. Well, it seems to me that if you're really determined to qualify, if only to spite your mother's doctor, you'd better free your mind from niggling worries and hates, or you'll never do it.'

Sally regarded her sombrely. 'How can you wash out everything that's worrying your mind? Is there a trick? If so, you'd better tell me. I need it.'

Cerise looked blank. 'I've never had my mind cluttered with anything like that. Oh, well, there was the big question of the family wanting me to come here, of course. But I grew up with a shrinking for the family obsession, nursing and all that. It was just the one thing to throw off. I found out that I could, so, on the principle of if-you-can't-beat-them-join-them, that's what I did, but that won't help you, will it?'

'It isn't like that, with me,' Sally agreed.

'Is it what you've been doing this last year since you left school?'

'You *are* polite!' Sally said, with a sudden snort of laughter. 'Oh, Oldham, you're growing on me! I shall finish up with you being my best friend. How awful for you!'

'I could think of worse fates,' said Cerise, laughing. 'All right, I gather you've been in disgrace this last year. Well, you give it way. You shy from the memory of it. Have you tried talking about it, getting it out of your system once and for all?'

Sally wrinkled her nose in distaste. 'No. I don't want to drag it out into the daylight. I just want to forget it, or at least bury it. Way down deep in my mind so I can forget it's there.'

Cerise brushed her hair and said, in a funny prissy voice intended to make Sally laugh, 'There's a theory shared by my mother and my aunt that that's the easiest way of losing your memory.'

Sally threw herself flat on her face on her bed, and laughed until she was breathless. 'But that's just what I'd *like* to do, you chump!'

'It can't be that bad, Marston, can it?' Cerise objected.

'Pretty bad,' Sally said shortly. 'After I got expelled, my school not being ready to put up with my habit of breaking bounds and climbing in windows after hours, I was found a job in a riding school. Well, that was all I could do – ride, and handle horses. They thought I might teach children to ride.'

'And did you?' Cerise asked, as Sally paused.

'No. I mucked out stables. Someone else had the job of teaching children, and in my humble opinion she wasn't any good.'

'But I wouldn't have thought you'd be the one to harbour jealousy or resentment over the allocation of a job,' Cerise murmured, in surprise.

'Who said I did?' Sally retorted. 'No, something happened – something rather nasty, to my way of thinking. Well, I just walked out of the job. Stupid, I suppose, but I haven't any patience with explaining, and I hate scenes. They're degrading ... with that sort of person.'

'The sort of person being Miss X., the nameless one who wasn't any good at teaching unfortunate children to ride?' Cerise twinkled.

'That's right. I hate her.'

'And you hate Roberta Nesbitt,' Cerise said, half to herself. 'Did something nasty happen in connection with her?'

'I think … I have no reason to think it, but instinct tells me I'm right … that she likes my father too much,' Sally said fastidiously.

'Oh! Does your mother know?'

'I haven't the ghost of an idea!' Sally said frankly. 'I sometimes think I don't know my mother very well, because she looks all serene, wrapped up in her happy safe world with my father, and yet she was shrewdly coming to the conclusion that all was not well with me, simply from the tone of my letters. And she never let on, not even to my father!'

Cerise stopped brushing her hair and looked thoughtfully at Sally. There was a lot being left unsaid, she decided, and she wisely refrained from asking Sally for any more. Much better leave Sally to offer information.

'So you left school under a cloud (isn't that a romantic way of putting it?) and had one job that misfired. Well, that's not so bad. Now, having talked about it, all you have to do is to concentrate on this job,' she said briskly.

'It isn't as easy as that,' Sally said in that abrupt tone that she used when she was embarrassed, bothered. 'Besides, if I want to keep friends with you (and I do!) I have to warn you about it now. It's men.'

Cerise shot her head up and looked frankly alarmed.

'Oh, don't look like that,' Sally said impatiently. 'What I mean is, I don't care about them – for a reason. I'm fed up with the lot of them. But oddly enough that seems to make them want to know me. I can't work it out and I couldn't care less, but the fact is, half the trouble I get into seems to be stemming from some girl deciding I've pinched her man-friend. So if you're keen on someone, either grab him quickly or keep him out of my sight.'

Cerise flushed. 'Men have not formed part of my existence so far. I have no reason to suppose they ever will.'

'Don't be a clot. Of course you'll get a man-friend. I don't know where they hid the men when we arrived, but I've seen quite a few around since then. Be like me – act as if they weren't there, and they come running.'

Cerise looked at Sally's glorious skin and

sparkling eyes, and for the briefest of seconds she envied Sally's glowing health and zest for life. That, she considered, was what the men must find irresistible.

She said, wrinkling her forehead, 'Thanks for all the pep talk, but if you can bring yourself back to your own problems for a moment, would it be in order for me to ask how you got into this hospital with a murky record like you'd have me believe you have?'

Sally grinned briefly. 'You know how. I've told you haven't I? Our dear G.P. is related to Matron.'

'Still, I wouldn't have thought she'd succumb to outside persuasions, unless you're trying to delude me into thinking your past is a lot worse than it is.'

Sally started to say something, then altered her mind. In the end she managed, 'Well, this is only a sort of trial period, isn't it, this twelve-week intensive patch? Plenty of time to weed out the doubtful material, I suppose, and I expect Sister Tutor and Home Sister are almost, if not quite, mind-readers! For all I know, they probably have scientific methods of getting the truth out of one, without one realising it.' But she wasn't really thinking of what she was saying. By then she was up on her feet, staring out of the window. 'Who's that down there?'

Cerise got up and joined her. Sally was watching a tall, rangy man in his early thirties, with a lick of dark hair, a long lean brown face and a big nose. He was standing hands I pockets, talking to Sister Tutor. Then he nodded briefly to her, smiled and left her.

But as he walked away, towards the front gate he must have felt that eyes were staring at him, for he looked up sharply, frowning. He couldn't see Sally's face from that distance, because of the light shining on the window pane, and after a minute he half shrugged and walked away.

'Is he on the staff, d'you suppose?' Sally murmured.

'Actually, yes,' Cerise said, in a muffled voice, and she turned away from the window. 'I saw him yesterday, and two seniors behind me were talking about him. I'm afraid he's beyond our reach, Marston.'

'Oldham, my infant, I may be only nineteen, but in my experience there isn't a man born who is beyond my reach if I wanted him badly enough. Who was that – one of the hospital Governors, then?'

'No,' said Cerise, plunging her confused face into cold water at the wash basin, and keeping the taps turned full on to make a noise and give her confidence. 'Actually it's John Weaver, the R.M.O.'

CHAPTER FOUR

Bruce Carmichael wrote once a week to Sally. He typed the letters, and signed them formally, but the tone of them was friendly enough. Cerise commented on them.

'He doesn't reciprocate your dislike, apparently, unless he has a large sense of duty, or a lot of time on his hands. Two full typed pages per week!'

'He's bossy and a putter-righter through and through,' said Sally. 'He thinks he can reform me. Last chance, indeed!'

'That really stung you, didn't it? Does he lecture you all through his letters?' Cerise asked idly. All her mail was from members of the family discussing hospital life as they knew it, comparing it with what she disclosed to them of the P.T.S. at Ventonbourne. No men wrote to her, unless one counted her grandfather, who had just given up general practice and missed it so badly that he had to talk about it to anyone who would listen.

'You can read them if you like,' said Sally, and threw the letters she had so far received across to Cerise. 'Go on, read them! You'll see what I mean! Absolutely innocuous, and no one would be surprised if he turned out to be my godfather, only he isn't.'

Cerise read the letters and looked nonplussed. 'He really likes you, doesn't he?' she said in surprise. 'I got the impression that it was quite the reverse.'

Sally shrugged. 'Well, he doesn't, or he wouldn't look at me like that.'

'Like what?'

'Like – oh, I don't know. As if he'd like to shake me. He firmly believes I'm to blame for my parents' state of health, you see,' and reluctantly she let out another bit of information – how her father had collapsed because of the dog tripping her mother. 'It even had to be the dog I'd been walking with, the dog who liked me. That's me all over – the most innocent things I do seem to get other people into trouble, and then I'm involved.'

'Still, the family doctor doesn't have to–' Cerise began, then she gave it up. It wasn't any use antagonising Sally, who clearly disliked him.

'He'll probably finish up with marrying Roberta,' Sally went on. 'Serve him right! Two bossy, efficient people. As a matter of fact, though, it would keep her from being too fond of my father. Oh, I don't know – no, I couldn't bear it if she were the wife of our G.P.'

She carefully painted her mouth with a discreet lipstick, then she confessed, grinning ruefully, 'If it were not for those two people, I might almost admit that I'm beginning to like training to be a nurse – but what an awful comedown for me, to finish up a pale imitation of dear Roberta.'

'It might please your parents!'

'No,' Sally said dully. 'I get the feeling that nothing I do now will ever please them. Come on, let's go if we're going – we don't want to find we've missed half the big picture!'

It was their evening out. They had one afternoon in, doing their studies, one evening out, and their afternoons alternated. Cerise and Sally usually went out together, but today they being joined by Mary Dane and Gay Leatherdale, the other two in their set who had the same times off.

The cinema was only five minutes' walk away from the hospital. The milk bar next door provided the fruit sundaes and hot chocolate they would have instead of tea when they came out, and next door to that was the big store where Mary was meaning to go in and search for a new purse and Gay, who was always bringing her nylons to disaster, wanted to get in a stock of a new cheap line she had heard were being advertised.

'What a madly exciting life student nurses lead!' Gay grinned, as they stopped outside to pool their resources for Mary to buy the tickets.

'But you wanted to be a nurse, didn't you?' Cerise couldn't resist saying. To her it was an affront on anyone's part to undertake a nurse's training without intending to finish it.

'I wanted some of the training,' Gay allowed. 'But I'm not going to stick out my life in a hospital.'

'Why ever not?' the others chorused.

'Because I want to be a newspaper-woman,' Gay said, and her irresponsible manner deserted her for a moment, to be replaced by the burning glint of ambition in her eyes. She was laughing again almost at once, but Sally had seen it there and wondered.

'What's that got to do with nursing?' Cerise asked blankly, as Mary joined them and they raced up to the circle in a huddle.

'I want as much experience of behind the scenes in different jobs as I can,' Gay explained seriously. 'My uncle's on a national newspaper and he said it gives a woman the best chance. A bit of nursing, a bit of rep. and modelling, a bit of teaching and a holiday job or two in shops or a factory. The lot! Then I'll know what I'm talking about if I have to write about any of those things. You never know when it will come in useful.'

They sat down in the back row of the circle, and Sally half listened to the others while they waited for the lights to go out. 'And a scandal in a hospital is the best story of all, but it's better if you know something of the life there,' Gay was saying.

'What on earth sort of scandal do you expect to find in a hospital?' Mary asked scornfully. 'You'd never find it out, anyway – that sort of thing is always hushed up. It isn't worth Matron's while to let a scandal leak. She's responsible for the nursing staff.'

Sally didn't hear what Cerise said about that. She was too busy wondering if anything in her own life was ever likely to leak out.

'Anyway, you'd have to have proof or you'd be in trouble yourself,' Mary snapped.

Gay, unperturbed, started to tell them an involved story of a girl in a convalescent home, as retold to her by her uncle, but Sally was concerned only by what Matron would have to say if anything came out of her past. Dr Bruce Carmichael had told Matron about the expulsion from school, in such a way as to suggest that Sally had been unlucky, and that it had been the only time. He didn't know, poor man, just how many times she had broken bounds before and thought nothing of it. The riding school he had glossed over as being an unfortunate experience which might very well have shaken Sally's nerves regarding horses for all time, and he knew very little about the hotel receptionist job and had referred to that very briefly as a holiday occupation.

As true as he knew, but she hadn't given him the whole truth, and if it ever came out it might put Matron in a very awkward position. Sally bit her lip, then shrugged it off. It was her business and no one else's, and if you liked to put it like that – well, she had had bad luck. She forgot the whole thing and settled to enjoy the film.

The others liked it, but long before it finished Sally felt her attention beginning to wander. The hero was vacuous and the heroine simply couldn't make up her mind between the two elderly men she had to choose from. Sally couldn't even feel sorry for her.

She leaned over and whispered to the enthralled Mary, and quietly went up the stairs to where the illuminated sign indicated the ladies' room. In there she took her time over re-making her face, and standing at the open window for a breath of air. She wondered what it was like to be riding over the downs with a string of small children on fat ponies behind her – her chosen profession, before she had been rudely jolted out of it. That same sky was over the downs near her old home, which someone else now occupied; it was over the riding school and Captain Philpotts and his pretty wife; it was over Iris Leame, too.

Why, she asked herself angrily, why think about that? The whole episode was closed, finished. Iris was teaching the children to ride (or trying to teach them!) and Captain Philpotts was still looking dotingly at his pretty blonde wife, and Mummy and Daddy were in France and Mummy was soon to have her operation, and Bruce Carmichael would type more long letters to her, and if Sally herself kept her head, she might turn out to be a passable nurse and never see any of them again. Her heart lurched at the thought of the possibility of her parents staying out of England for always, but better that, perhaps, than to be near enough to Sally to keep asking her, in open disbelief, what had really happened at the Philpotts' place.

Better, too, than to have them come back and find out about Frank Sandford…

She idly let her glance drop to the car park below where a man was trying to back a big car out of a small space in the absence of the car park attendant. It looked like the car Frank Sandford used to drive. As the driver's head came into view, and he slowly but expertly got out of his predicament, Sally nearly fell out of the window in surprise. It couldn't be! How could it be Frank, here, of all places? No, it was someone just like him, and she had been thinking of him, and thought it was him.

But it was. There was no doubt of it, when he got out of the car and walked all round to inspect the damage, if any. That was Frank's tall figure, his good tailoring, the way he did his hair, the way he threw his head back at last, a little with satisfaction, a little with triumph. With inches to spare, and he hadn't touched his precious car anywhere at all!

Sally came in from the window, feeling sick. She closed her eyes, and told herself not to be a fool. It … was … not … Frank. *It couldn't be!*

When she opened her eyes again he was gone, and so was the big car. She leaned out, unbelieving, but there was no sign of it. Already a land-rover was manoeuvring into that space, and there was a tinkle of glass as he touched the car behind and smashed his backing light. At once there was the sound of feet running; the car park attendant appeared, and the owner of the other car. Their raised voices drifted up. Other cars came in, and more people.

The door of the ladies' opened. Mary said, 'Oh, there you are! What's the matter? You look white as a sheet! We thought you couldn't be well!'

And behind her, Gay said, 'Is she here? Come on, Marston, it's time to go! We've got to rush if we want any grub.'

Sally shook her head. 'You all go on. I'll follow – I don't feel so good.'

They leaned out of the window to see what she was looking at, and presumed there had been an accident.

'You'll have to get used to that, Marston. They say we might be sent to Casualty sooner than usual.'

She nodded absently, and they left her, shouting where she could find them when she felt better.

She took her time, then drifted downstairs after them. She would have to, sooner or later, so she might as well join them now, but it was true – she did feel sick. The smell of the soup and hot chocolate would finish her. She felt sick because she had seen Frank and he had apparently forgotten all about her.

Or had he? She smartened her pace. The chances were she might see him somewhere, and at least ask him why he had walked out on her like that.

Some boys rushed up the stairs, cannoned into her, knocked her flying. She picked herself up, but her own mad rush had been stopped, and now she had time to think. Where would she find him? He had been leaving, not parking. And anyway, could she see herself asking him that? she taunted herself derisively. Get a hold on yourself, Sally Marston, she told herself angrily. He's gone. Let him go, if he wants to.

She felt dreadful. Her head was pounding and she didn't want to go back to the Nurses' Home with the other three, or listen to their happy chatting about their nylons or the film, what they had had at the milk bar, or what they thought of Gay's life on a national newspaper. She just wanted to creep into some dark place and cry, because she had fallen in love too soon, and not known how much to give or to keep back. She had given her heart, and it hadn't really been wanted.

Where was the sense of it all? What did people want to fall in love for, anyway? She remembered the first time she had seen Frank Sandford. He had been looking in complete frustration at a puncture, below the school wall. He had kicked the wheel of his beloved car, and she, sitting on top of the wall, had laughed at him. And he had looked up at her... The first man to look at her and really see her as a young woman of rising eighteen, not as a girl in a finishing school with a talent for being a nuisance to authority.

Sally looked round for a chemist. She must get something for this headache. She could, of course, wait till she went back to the Nurses Home, but Home Sister would fuss over her and want to take her temperature, and everyone would want to know what was wrong with her. Such a fuss about a headache, which she knew perfectly well wasn't the symptom of impending infection, but a headache which inevitably came with suppressed tears and wretchedness over indulging in unhappy memories.

She shot into the chemist's and asked for something for her headache, and he insisted on mixing a draught for her. He went to the back of the shop, and she prowled around looking at colour slides on a stand.

Someone came in the door as she came out from behind the stand. She almost crashed into him. He put out his hands to steady her, and as he touched her she tingled all over and her legs felt too unsteady to hold her.

'*Sally!*' said Frank, his voice a rising question, unable to take it in that it was really her. 'It *is* you, isn't it? What on earth are you doing in Ventonbourne?'

She couldn't answer. She wasn't in uniform and she couldn't think of anything to say. She just looked at him, her head tilted back to meet his height. Before the startled eyes of the chemist holding out his little medicine glass of cloudy white liquid, Frank gathered Sally into his arms and kissed her.

'Well, bless me, perhaps you won't need this now,' said the chemist, and took it back with him to the dispensary.

Frank held her away from him and looked at her. She reddened, furious with herself for such a display of emotion. 'I didn't expect to see you!' she flared.

He smiled, in that well-remembered way, and she saw to her dismay that he was every bit as handsome, as self-assured, and as tender as she remembered him. 'Let's get out of here,' she muttered, and marched over to the counter and put down some money to cover the cost of the draught she now no longer needed. She was walking on air and she couldn't stop herself from elating. Her heavy headache had gone, and the clock had leapt back a year, to the time when she had been waiting for Frank and he hadn't turned up; the time before her expulsion from school, her mother's accident, her father's illness, the time before Roberta had come into her life, the people at the riding school, the people at the Wishing Well Hotel. Her eyes glowed as she came away from the counter, and there was a faint flush in her golden cheeks that touched her good looks to sheer beauty.

'What are you doing here, Frank?' she repeated.

'Just passing through, m'dear,' he said easily, taking her arm as if it were a year ago, and not today, with three hundred and sixty-five days of heartache and hurt between them. 'Not looking for you, certainly, because I hadn't a clue where to find you. What happened to you?'

It wasn't any use saying curtly that she had been expelled for being out late, and with him. Frank wouldn't care for that at all. She said instead, 'Much water under the bridge. I'm at hospital now, training to be a nurse.'

'Good heavens!' he said faintly, but he wasn't really interested. He really wanted to tell her about himself. 'I was waiting for you, when a chappie came round the corner in a magnificent Alpha – low-slung, white, a beauty, and he didn't pick that up for fifty quid, I do assure you. In fact, he didn't pick it up for a penny. He helped himself to it, as it was discovered later. And he had knocked someone down and not stopped.'

'Oh, no!' said Sally, enthralled with the story. She hated herself for it, but Frank could always make a narrative breathtaking. 'What happened?'

He shrugged. 'He'd knocked down one chappie, so what was another, between friends? Luckily, he only pipped me on the shoulder as he skidded up on to the pavement. In a bit of a hurry, he was, actually, and like a clot I got in the way. But the blow shot me backwards – the old feet weren't nippy enough – and I fell back against the wall, knocking myself out. Well, I came to in hospital and I was told it was a different date on the calendar. Concussed for almost a week. Worried sick about you. Dared not write to you on account of your school censoring letters–'

'Opening them,' she corrected him swiftly, 'if they didn't come from one's home town.'

'I should have remembered that, and written to a chappie I know to post it from your home town, except that I'd lost your address in the scrum. That was why I couldn't write to you later, when I'd heard from some gardener bloke that you'd been expelled. Well, I could hardly call at the front door of your school and give the maid my hat and stick and say I'd called on Miss Sally Marston, now could I?'

That made her giggle – a little light-headedly, it was true, but that was the effect Frank had always had on her. And now here he was back, with a valid (if colourful) reason for not having met her that day, nor having contacted her since.

'And then one day, last week actually, I found your home address and took the bull by the horns and dropped in, but it was shut up, empty, and sold, so a neighbour told me. New people coming in soon.'

'Already?' she said faintly. 'Our doctor arranged the sale, to another of his patients. He might have told me! That shows you how you can trust people.'

'Well, have a heart, m'dear, he might only have just fixed it up himself. These people were pretty woolly about dates and things. I took myself off, but quick. I'd got sunglasses on, but you never know – they might have recognised something else about me next time.'

'Why do you always want to avoid being recognised?' she asked unthinkingly. She was so happy, she wasn't being guarded in what she said.

The corner of his mouth turned up, in a way she had forgotten. Just for a second, then he was smiling again and he had replaced the dark glasses, although it was too late in the day for any really strong sunshine.

'Silly-billy, to protect your reputation, of course! You're a very young, tender scrap, and I'm a wicked old man – well, past my first flush of youth, shall we say? I don't want to have to face angry male relatives until I'm ready to declare my intentions, now do I?'

Her heart did sickening leaps of joy and excitement and her voice wouldn't work, but she could whistle, and she did – a silly little tune she had always whistled when she was happy.

He remembered it, of course. 'You still do that! That's my girl, get your happiness out of your system before you have to go back to your job. Is that the hospital there?' he asked, as she pointed to a side road and they turned the corner. 'Good grief, it looks like an Army barracks. What were your parents thinking of? Where are they now, by the way? Not in this town?'

He sounded just a little apprehensive as he said it. Sally quickly reassured him. 'They're in France. In Switzerland, soon, because Mummy has to have an operation. Train crash. Hurt her legs.' Keep it brief, she told herself. Frank never could bear the gory details.

'And you really consented to be a nurse? Have you really given it any thought, m'dear? I mean, pretty distasteful job, what? I say, you won't be tempted to tell me about it next time we meet, will you? I'd hate it.'

Her heart leapt. So he was going to meet her again! She could afford to make a joke of it – she had to, in fact, to decently clothe her excitement. 'What would you hate – the details or meeting me?'

He looked down into her dancing eyes. 'You know very well which part of it I wouldn't hate,' he said softly. 'When's it going to be – this next meeting of ours? How much free time do you get?'

She told him. 'Three hours a day, alternating afternoon and evening, and one day a week.'

'Keep all your free time for me,' he commanded. 'How do I contact you?'

'At the Nurses' Home, but write to me as your niece, in case they steam them open. I wouldn't put that past them!'

'Oh, dear, must I be an uncle? Very well, then. I shall try to act the part with flair. Goodbye, m'dear. Give me a niecely kiss,' and he tilted her face and kissed her forehead – an odd little kiss that left her filled with wild longing, and curiously as disturbed as if he had kissed her full on the mouth.

She hurried back to the Home. She was late, and there would be trouble. She couldn't even spare a second to look back and wave to him, as she used to do. She had trouble to face.

Her friends had covered for her, however,

by telling Home Sister and Sister Tutor that Sally had been unwell and missed half the film, and that she had gone in search of a chemist instead of going to eat with them.

Home Sister wasn't pleased. 'Really, nurse, don't you know yet that the thing to do in such a circumstance is to come straight back and report to me?' She put a cool dry hand on Sally's hot forehead. 'H'm, flushed and hot. What pills did you buy? Don't you know yet that that isn't allowed here?'

'Sorry, Sister,' Sally mumbled, and wondered how much Frank had sent her temperature soaring. 'Actually the chemist made up a draught for me, but it was late and I didn't have it. I left it on the counter.' Not strictly true, but not a falsehood, she comforted herself.

'Good gracious, and ran all the way back, I suppose!' Home Sister scolded. 'I shall have to arrange for a lecture especially on what to do if overcome with indisposition while out, I can see! What the mothers of you girls have been about, not to brief you properly on such elementary situations, I cannot think.'

Cerise flushed. She hated people to tilt, however unwittingly, at her mother, but she was too well brought up to point out that in her case it didn't apply. She stood and listened to Home Sister's homily while Sally escaped to the sick bay, where she promptly fell asleep to dream of Frank Sandford.

She was still a little giddy in her manner the next day, but as two nurses went down with 'flu, Home Sister allowed Sally to get up, if only to escape from the more virulent germs. Sally found there was a letter waiting for her from Frank.

'Dear Niece,' it read, 'I have some tickets for a nice wholesome show in Queenswood which I am sure even your parents would approve of, so I shall expect you to be ready for me in good time at the gates of the Nurses' Home this evening. Don't keep me waiting, there's a good child. Show this to the authorities if they are as protective of your welfare as I hope they are. (signed) Uncle Faithful.'

If ever there was a tongue-in-cheek letter, this was it, Sally thought, uncertain whether to collapse in gales of hysterical giggles, or to be indignant at the way in which he had elected to openly dupe the authorities. In the end, for safety's sake she did show it to Home Sister, who was curiously pleased with it. She believed it was the genuine uncle-ish letter, and approved of the whole thing.

Sally also showed Cerise. She had to show

someone, or else she would have burst with happiness, and she knew she could trust Cerise.

'What's the excitement for, over an uncle?' Cerise asked blankly.

Sally threw herself flat on her face on her bed and grasped the sides of it until the knuckles showed white. She was shaking all over and she turned a confused and flushed face to Cerise, to say, 'He is *not* my uncle. Anything but!'

Slow colour stained Cerise's face. 'I hope you know what you're doing,' she said at last. Such excitement shown openly over a man was unseemly, to say the least, and offended Cerise as she had imagined it would offend Sally from what little she knew of her. 'I thought you were off men,' she added crossly.

Sally choked, 'I was, with him particularly, because I thought he'd let me down. After all, in waiting for him that day, I got back late and was expelled from school.'

'And?' Cerise asked flatly.

'And now I see how hasty I was in coming to such a conclusion, because he's told me today why he couldn't meet me as arranged.'

'The story will be a good one,' Cerise hazarded, blunt common sense taking the place of any worldly wisdom the other

P.T.S. babes might have had.

Sally flushed. 'It's the truth!' she flared, and because Cerise had questioned its validity, she told her just what the explanation had been.

Cerise was still unconvinced. 'Fortuitous,' she muttered, but Sally didn't catch that, because now she was bouncing off the bed to go through her clothes to see what she could wear.

'Something a niece would wear to meet her uncle and see a nice wholesome show,' Cerise reminded her quickly.

'Oh, blow! Then it had better be this plain, plain thing that incidentally almost broke the bank,' Sally decided, bringing out a light blue dress that she had always regarded as a mistake. 'I wanted to wear this black suit. It's got a bag to go with it with a mink bow on the flap. Are you sure I can't–?'

'Oh, help, quite sure!' Cerise said hurriedly. 'Even Home Sister would have doubts if she saw you going to meet Uncle in that thing! Be your age, Marston!'

She regarded Sally with new eyes. Sally looked older than her nineteen years at this moment. She had the confident glow of the girl who has a man who admires her; a girl, moreover, Cerise suspected, who was used to men admiring her, even if she didn't particularly want their admiration. It did things to a girl, Cerise saw, and she sighed. 'What show will he take you to? Do you know?'

'No, but I don't know of a wholesome show running in Queenswood at the moment and I'm prepared to stake the little I posses on the fact that my Frank would never go to a wholesome show if his life depended on it. I expect it will be a roadhouse – you know, cabaret sort of thing. Certainly not something at the Empire for family consumption.'

'What time do you expect to get back from that sort of thing?' Cerise asked blankly. 'You haven't forgotten you have to be in by ten, I suppose?'

Sally sat down suddenly. 'I had, you know! Well, I shall have to look around for a convenient window, won't I?'

'No, Marston! No, don't start that business again! Please, no! I'd do anything for you, but not get involved in something that would ruin my chances of finishing my training here. Besides, it's such a stupid thing to do.'

Sally struggled with her rising temper and didn't flare out at Cerise. She liked her too much to risk losing her allegiance. 'Don't worry,' she said shortly. 'I won't involve you. What I've done before, I can do again.'

Nothing Cerise would say would make Sally alter her mind, until in the end, goaded, Sally agreed, 'All right, I'll scrap the show idea and let him take me for a drive instead. We shall be back on time, but I would be safer watching a floor show with him, believe me!'

Cerise was left very unhappy, but she sat the evening through, working on her notes with determination.

But the hours of the clock on the bookcase crawled past ten o'clock, and reluctantly, at Lights Out, Cerise untidied Sally's bed, laid her day clothes out in the way Sally usually left them, and hid Sally's night things, dressing gown and slippers, so that it would appear Sally had been to bed but had got out again to go down the passage. She hated herself for stooping to this, but at least it wasn't sinking so low as to put the bolster in the bed, that Sally had once flippantly told her was the case at her old school.

As Cerise had anticipated, Home Sister merely poked her head round the door, clucked at the sight of Sally's bed, and went out again. Cerise prayed Sally would get in all right.

Sally didn't come back until midnight. As she stood looking at the window that was supposed to have been left open for her, and which quite clearly was not, she felt sick. This was how it had been before, when she had been expelled from school. As she stood there, debating whether to go straight round to the front and knock to be let in, she was aware of a rush of grief at the thought of leaving this place. She had been here a matter of a fortnight, and she found she would hate to leave it.

While she was facing that surprising thought, someone came along softly on the grass behind her – a tall man, one she recognised in the moonlight as the man Cerise had said was the R.M.O., John Weaver.

Sally assessed him in that first really close look. She knew men well enough to know she could trust this one, so she determined on her line, the frank and open one.

'Oh, dear, caught!' she murmured. 'Sorry, sir. I was going round the front to knock at the door.'

'Then I'd better walk you round, hadn't I, nurse, in case your longing look at that window incites it to open of its own volition and invite you to climb up.'

There was a hint of laughter in his voice, and he was keeping his voice down, she noticed.

She agreed with him and started to walk away. He kept beside her. 'You're new, aren't you? What's your name?'

'Marston, sir. Sally Marston.'

'Ah, well, with a name like that, I'm not surprised to find you in trouble. Is your story good?'

Sally was taken aback. She was tempted to tell him who she had been out with, just for the fun of seeing how he took it, because it didn't really matter now. Her future was doomed. Last chance, you didn't last long, she told herself grimly.

With the words 'last chance', the memory of Bruce Carmichael rose before her, and her fighting blood was up. She was still angry with him for not having told her the news about the sale of the house having been completed.

'I was out with my uncle,' she said shortly.

'Come now, you'll have to do better than that,' said Dr Weaver, his eyebrows shooting up.

'Don't you believe me?' she demanded.

'I have yet to see the uncle who could make a girl's feet literally leave the ground, and her eyes glitter like stars,' he said dryly.

Sally cursed what Frank could do to her, to make it so obvious to everyone else.

Frank had kissed her so much tonight that she wasn't in a fit state to think.

And then, to add to her troubles, Home Sister walked briskly across from the other direction, and stopped short in front of them.

'Well, Nurse Marston, I think it very inconsiderate of your uncle to keep you out as late as this, after writing such a nice little note requesting permission.'

Sally glanced at the R.M.O., whose jaw had dropped.

'What made him keep you out so late, nurse?' Home Sister went on.

'His new car broke down, Sister, and he was livid. Because I laughed, I expect. Anyway, to make matters worse, we couldn't find a taxi, and he brought me back by train and bus. He didn't like that.'

'I shouldn't think he did! Well, I can't let this go unreported, but as it wasn't your fault, we shall have to see.' She hesitated, puzzled at a faint memory of something that wasn't quite right. For the moment, the rumpled bed eluded her, because the R.M.O. was standing there with such an odd expression on his face as he looked down at Sally.

Sally said goodnight and escaped, glad to have got off with no more than that. If there had been a sizeable lecture, she might have lost her temper. She always did, when she had something nice she wanted to dream over and she was prevented from escaping by a lecture.

Cerise was more put out than she was. She awoke at the sound of Sally's return and wanted to hear all about it. She had heard the voices below her window, but hadn't heard what was said.

Sally reported the whole thing with gusto and missed the point when Cerise burst out: 'But what am I going to do about your bed? Look what I did to it, and Home Sister *saw* it! She'll remember that!'

Sally wasn't unduly put out. She was ripping her clothes off, slinging them all over the place, and she shot into bed without bothering to wash. She wanted to dream of Frank and his tenderness tonight.

'Was it true?' Cerise insisted. 'All that about his car breaking down and coming back by train and bus?'

'His car certainly broke down,' Sally allowed, and not another word was to be got out of her then.

Cerise slept badly and awoke with dark circles round her eyes, from worrying. But nothing was said to either of them.

'That certainly *is* funny,' Sally agreed with

her when they talked it over after their release from the classroom that day. 'You don't suppose the R.M.O. put in a good word for me, do you? He was looking at me in a very odd manner. I think he's rather a sweetie.'

'Tell me again just what he said,' Cerise demanded.

Sally did, without frills. She was so used to the admiration of men that she didn't need to dress the story up. She told it so baldly that Cerise knew it was the truth this time, even if Sally had suppressed some of the truth about the reason for her being late last night.

'What do you think, Oldham? It wouldn't be possible for any R.M.O. to cover for a girl, or persuade the authorities not to kick her out, or her friend for covering her tracks, surely? It doesn't sound feasible.'

'I wouldn't have thought so,' agreed Cerise. 'Unless ... unless the R.M.O. put in a plea for clemency because it was the first offence. He might, especially if Home Sister really believed that story about it being your uncle. Yes, I suppose he just might have,' she said wretchedly.

Sally looked surprised at her tone. 'Then buck up, my old pal! You won't be out on your ear for messing up my bed and leading poor old Home Sister to think the obvious!'

she said rallyingly.

Cerise didn't answer. She couldn't be sure, of course, but it seemed likely to her that that nice Dr John Weaver was probably joining the ranks of the other men who slipped under Sally's spell.

CHAPTER FIVE

There was another letter from Dr Bruce Carmichael that day. It cut the ground from beneath Sally's feet by telling her about the sale of the house. He had apparently been waiting for the whole thing to be confirmed before he had told her, and if she had been in the mood to judge the tone of the letter, she would have seen clearly that he was trying to let her down lightly about closing her old home so quickly. He thought that she had liked the place and regretted deeply being thrown out of it so suddenly.

Sally, who was waiting to meet Frank Sandford when she read that letter, was in no mood to look for hidden niceties. She stood at the bus stop on the main road to London, waiting for Frank to rip into sight in that car of his, that seemed to eat up the miles, and she forced herself to think of other things so that she shouldn't notice that he was already half an hour late and that he had let her down before.

The last two times she had been with Frank, he had been so sweet. He had talked sadly of his life and of how happiness had just seemed to elude him but that he was hoping that in the not so distant future he would have the right to the happiness he firmly believed came to every man if he was patient enough. 'And,' he had finished, looking at Sally in a very meaning way, 'the right of every woman, too.'

Sally tried not to let herself believe he was implying that he was intending marriage to her. He had implied that before, just before he had gone away. Anyway, this time it was different, she comforted herself. She was no longer at school, where she couldn't get out alone to meet a man. Besides, she was over a year older now than on that other occasion. And anyway, he was now staying for some time in the district.

She allowed herself to think of his kisses, that last night she had been with him, when she had got caught by the R.M.O., and she purposely didn't let herself dwell on the fact that this was not the first time he had caused her to be caught, out after hours.

She felt a little sick as she dragged herself back from the memory of his embrace, and realised that it was a great deal later and he still hadn't come.

Shame, because she was still apparently as putty in his hands, was replaced by the soaring temper that had got her into trouble on many occasions. Black rage, not that he should treat her like this, but that she should still be so stupid over him, took possession of her, and she turned swiftly to walk back the way she had come. Not to the hospital, to face Cerise's embarrassed questioning look at her early return, but to the town, anywhere, where she could either pick up a bus and ride around until it was too late to stay out any longer, or to find some café that was still open, to sit idling over a coffee.

A car that was vaguely familiar slowed down and edged into the kerb, keeping pace with her. She was about to ignore it, but the R.M.O. stuck his head out and said, 'Hi!'

That made her jump and she went back to him.

'You and I seem to meet in very odd circumstances,' he said. 'This is really no place for a P.T.S. babe. Any use asking what you're doing here at this time of the evening?'

She glared at him. His reference to where he had seen her last, outside the Nurses' Home after midnight, vainly trying to get in through a window, was, she considered, a blow beneath the belt, and unworthy of the R.M.O.

'I've been stood up for a date!' she muttered, but her face was so stormy that it made him laugh.

'You do see life, don't you?' he chuckled. 'What are you going to do with yourself now – or shouldn't I run the risk of asking? Oh, come on, get in! I'll take you anywhere you want to go. I'm not doing anything much. Yes, I insist on your getting into my car, where I can keep an eye on you for the next five minutes. You look ready to murder someone.'

Sally got in. Quite suddenly she was tired, and rather bewildered. Cerise, who was unsophisticated and had had no experience of men friends whatever, could have told Sally that Frank Sandford (if she could have seen him) was not a man to trust with one's future, nor a man to appreciate a girl like Sally giving him her heart, because Sally's way of giving was to literally throw the gift, with all the force of her generous nature. But then Cerise didn't know Frank Sandford and hadn't even had the opportunity of seeing him, and her friendship was too short with Sally to allow her to feel she could take many liberties by way of giving advice.

Sally fretted about where she had gone wrong, and her young face was so mutinous and hurt that the R.M.O. quietly turned off the motorway and away from the direction of the hospital and drove off out into the quiet country roads, in the hope that Sally would ease out.

'I remember,' he said in a conversational voice, 'a young cousin of mine once looking just like you do now.'

Sally restrained herself from saying something quite rude about his young cousin, and sat very still.

He continued, 'She had had a very bad patch altogether. Constantly in trouble. No one seemed to understand her. And she hadn't a great fund of words to tell anyone who wanted to know just what had gone wrong.'

Sally glanced at him, without much interest. Common sense told her that if the R.M.O. was in the mood to give confidences, she really ought to be a little more polite to him. After all, he didn't really have to go out of his way to help any young nurse.

'What happened to her?' she managed.

'Oh, well, it got worse before it got better, but in the end she found some nice chap who married her and now she's just had her first. Silly girl, all for the want of telling someone her troubles, and giving someone a chance to straighten them out.'

'Who did straighten them out for her?' Sally asked then, with real curiosity.

'No one, actually. They sorted themselves out.'

'Then they couldn't have been as bad as mine,' she said flatly. 'I don't see how anyone can straighten out my life.'

'Now that's either a bit of childish showing-off, a sweeping generalisation because you feel in a hating mood, or it's true, and if it's the latter case, then I really think someone ought to lend a hand before it's too late. Which is it?'

She hesitated. Somehow she couldn't bring herself to tell him of the awful things she had got mixed up in, during the past year. She found herself thinking that if she could tell anyone that at all, it would be Bruce Carmichael. She couldn't think why and she felt a sense of shock at the discovery of that, but in the end she decided that it was because

Bruce was their local G.P. and knew the family so well in all its moods and circumstances. After all, in spite of a man's youth, if he has been responsible for dragging you up from the depths when you were almost out cold with a particularly nasty 'bug' that had made you feel like death, you couldn't look on him as a stranger any more. Nor as a man, either, she thought, frowning, as she remembered his good looks and the way other people went in a flap over them. How could you think of a doctor as a man you might be interested in, if he had examined you, seen you without make-up and looking like nothing on earth, in a tumbled maelstrom that had once been silk sheets and neat cornered blankets, your eyes heavy and dark shadows beneath; a miserable sick thing that might be a creature of any age, but certainly not a girl who normally looked like something off a glossy magazine cover? No, Bruce Carmichael had seen her with her back hair down. If anyone at all should discover the unfortunate details of this past year, it would have to be him, and no other man.

So she said shortly to the R.M.O., 'The first!'

He wasn't, however, entirely convinced. She might insist that it was a bit of showing-off until the cows came home, but he had his own ideas about that.

He said, 'Well, I'll take your word for it, but if you don't mind, I must find somewhere to eat. I'm starving. Will you join me, or must I take you back to the hospital before I find that meal?'

She discovered she, too, was starving. It wasn't right to consider such hunger, when she had been breaking her heart over Frank's again leaving her in the lurch not so long ago, but then anger was predominant at the moment; grief would come later.

'I'm hungry, too,' she said.

'That's what I like about a young woman,' he remarked cheerfully, swinging away to creep down a narrow lane that really wouldn't take any other traffic but his own big car. 'A nice brevity, leaving one in no uncertainty about what she wants. Most girls go all round the world to get at what they want to say, and after one has found out, one is too tired to care.'

She laughed, unwillingly, and just then a turn in the lane revealed an ancient inn, standing well back before a triangle of grass, with a sagging tiled roof and splendid rafters; an inn that was a great deal larger than it looked, when one got a view of the back of it.

'I've discovered quite a few of these old coaching inns,' he remarked. 'Of course, they're not old through and through. Someone's had a go at them, and eradicated dry rot and woodworm, but the restoration has been skilfully done, and now they trade on their name for good food as much as for wines and spirits. Do they allow you to drink wine, at home?'

She coloured. Frank had taught her many things about wine, and other men had taught her the delights of rum and old brandy. Instinct told her that the R.M.O. wouldn't appreciate such an early education, however, so she said, 'If you mean the table wines of France, my parents have allowed that.' She had no conscience about it, either, because the R.M.O. was nothing to her, as friends went: he represented law and order, and she was already dangerously near the edge of that, so it was up to her to keep on the right side of the line without necessarily diverging from the truth.

He turned out to be good company and soon had her laughing, and then he said, with one of those sudden darts in conversation that were so disconcerting to her, 'Did the last man you went out with entertain you in this way?'

Frank entertained like no one else. Frank had the waiters eating out of his hand, and usually he didn't go in for small coaching inns but very nice restaurants and hotels. He was rather conventional about eating habits, Sally thought.

She shook her head, and was uncomfortably aware that the R.M.O. was watching her all the time, and considering, reading her thoughts almost.

'You look,' he said, 'as if you're trying to enjoy eating with me, but the ghost of the other chap is sitting between us. Right?'

'Have you never had a ghost at a meal before?' she countered.

'You're too young to say things like that or to know about them,' he told her severely. 'And yet you're not young in the way the other P.T.S. babes are. I can't quite decide how you seem to me.' He frowned, and she writhed under his searching look. 'I think you look touchingly young until one realises that it's only a veneer. The others don't look so young and then one realises that they're terribly unsophisticated and inexperienced, as of course they should be, at that age. You know, I wish you'd tell me what you've been up to.'

'You know, Dr Weaver, I'm tempted to do just that,' she said softly.

'To try to shock me? I don't shock easily.'

'No, to see just how much of it you believed, only there's a risk. You might just be as cussed as I am, and decide to believe it all, but then you'd have to go to Matron with the story and then I'd be thrown out, and I'd hate that.'

'You want to be a nurse so badly?' he frowned. Clearly he found that very difficult to believe.

'No, not terribly badly,' she had the honesty to admit. 'But someone has said that this is to be my last chance, and if I get thrown out and give him the right to jeer and be so beastly triumphant as only he can be, I shall never be able to forgive myself.'

'Oh.' The R.M.O. pulled a face. 'Not the best reason for becoming a nurse. I take it that this is the man who is occupying all your waking thoughts? The man in your life!'

Sally looked astonished. 'Good gracious, no! It's just our family doctor but he's so bombastic, so pleased with himself, so right all the time, and so scornful of everyone else, that I'd just like to prove him wrong this once, just this once!'

Like Cerise, the R.M.O. looked very oddly at her. 'Tell me, what is this chap like? Do I know him – what's his name?'

'His name is Dr Bruce Carmichael,' she said angrily.

'Carmichael? But we had a Carmichael here, oh, let's see, how many years ago would it be? His name, I recall, was Bruce. Quite a coincidence, because he'd be a fairly young chap.'

'I know, and I've been told till I'm sick of hearing about it how he trained at your hospital. Oh, yes, it's the same one all right.'

'Oh.' Those 'oh's' of the R.M.O were weighty with varying shades of meaning, she thought furiously. She wished he would think of some other ejaculation.

'Anyway, I am *not* going to give him the satisfaction of seeing me thrown out,' she went on.

'He's a cousin of Matron, I believe,' the R.M.O. said mildly, but his eyes were twinkling. 'Now I begin to see why you weren't thrown out the other night.' He traced patterns in the tablecloth. 'It was no uncle, I imagine?'

She just sat glaring at him.

'The same chap who stood you up tonight, in fact?'

Speechless and miserable, she sat silently watching him. He was a long time making those patterns and finally he rubbed the back of his head, and he said, 'I've got myself into a bit of a spot, it seems, wouldn't you agree with me?'

'I don't know what you mean, sir.'

'Come now, don't be sullen with me. That isn't worthy of you. You must see how I'm placed. I can hardly go to Matron about you since her own cousin edged you in, but at the same time I really can't be quiet about this, since you led poor Home Sister to think you were out with your uncle.'

'He wrote to me and I showed her the letter, and he sounded just like my uncle. Otherwise I wouldn't have been able to go out with him. But there was no harm in it.'

'There seems to be quite a lot of harm in it, and I'm as deeply in the muck as you are by sheer implication. As I see it, the only way for us is for me to listen to a full confession from you.'

'I'd much rather just clear out,' she said baldly. 'The end product would be the same, without disclosing what I've been up to.'

'Not necessarily,' and again his lips twitched. She made him laugh when he ought to be being very severe with her. 'I just want to know what happened during the past year.'

He was tenacious. He was also the R.M.O. and not nearly so vulnerable to trouble as he would have her think. The devil in her drove her to take him at his word and tell him, if only to see just how he would wriggle out of the position such a confession would really put him in.

'All right, I'll tell you. By a series of unfortunate accidents or twists of Fate (call them what you like!) I found myself in possession of a diamond necklace worth a fortune. I got rid of it at once, instinctively, of course, but someone saw what I did with it, and then I was involved in cheating insurance companies.'

His smile vanished and she quailed before the black anger that flooded his face.

Then the thunderous look melted away and he laughed, rather uncomfortably. 'I asked for that!' he said, and the more he thought about it, the more it appeared to amuse him. 'As if you would be likely to give a confidence because someone ordered you to! Still, you didn't have to be quite so dramatic in cooking up a story, did you?'

A faint smile touched her mouth. 'I was in love,' she said simply. 'I'm also impetuous. The rest is sheer bad luck and a total incapability for watching the time.'

'That's better! Now that I can believe! I suppose you just got chucked out of everywhere you alighted on that score alone.'

She nodded. 'I don't suppose you've been in love, Dr Weaver. I expect you're far too sensible to let yourself do any such thing. I merely mentioned it because if you'd been in love you would know how stupid it can make a person who is normally fairly responsible.

He liked that. He nodded. 'That I can also understand. We'll overlook the first bit of nonsense. I understand it's quite an amusing pastime for young nurses to try to pull the poor old R.M.O.'s leg, especially if the opportunity is handed to them on a plate as it was with you. But now I quite see your point, and if you'll be a sensible girl and try to forget the chap, I'll make a bargain with you. I'm quite good at being forgetful if I want to forget anything, such as a very personal confidence given to me.'

The meal ended very amicably, and he took her for another pleasant little drive before he drove back to the Nurses' Home.

The next day Sally was off in the afternoon. Cerise said, 'I suppose you're going out with one of your friends?'

Sally was still smarting over Frank. He

had sent a note bitterly regretting that he hadn't been able to keep his appointment with her, and that he wouldn't be able to see her today either, as he had been called away on business. She was just going to tell Cerise that she was free to go to the pictures with her if she liked when the letter from Bruce Carmichael fell out of her pocket.

She stopped to pick it up and remembered the tailpiece. 'Blow, I can't come out with you, Cerise. Our flipping family doctor is coming. I'd forgotten. I suppose he'll stick around for the whole three hours and insist on bringing me back again.' She glanced out of the window. 'Talk of the devil, there he is now! And he's got a new car. How does he do it?'

Cerise joined her and they stared down at the big dark car edging into the drive. It was large, new, just missing being too prosperous-looking. Sally didn't know it, but he had already been to see his cousin, Miss York, and had just driven round from that door. Matron's office had been in a flutter about him because he was so handsome.

Cerise commented on that, too, as he suddenly flicked a glance up at the windows of the Nurses' Home before getting out of his car.

Sally stared down at him with new eyes. She had always been furious with him because he was so good-looking, but she hadn't remembered he was quite so handsome, quite so debonair. It didn't seem right for an unmarried local G.P. to be so glamorous-looking. Well, it would cause a flutter among the P.T.S. girls all right. Her life wouldn't be worth living for a while, because of the speculation.

'Here goes,' she said, hastily picking up a raincoat and her shoulder bag. 'It doesn't do to keep him waiting.'

'Not even while you change into something pretty?' Cerise murmured. There had been a desperate amount of selecting of clothes and making-up, for the man who had called himself Sally's uncle

Sally reddened as she read Cerise's thoughts. 'Not likely! We shall bicker all the time, and why bother to make up for someone who's going to scold you?'

Cerise watched her go, with a puzzled frown. She had already heard about the episode of the R.M.O. Sally had been rather frustrated because Cerise had said nothing about it, but Cerise could find nothing to say. There had been a wild longing inside her to be that girl, Sally Marston, who by her very inability to keep out of trouble had aroused the protective instincts in yet another man – the R.M.O.

Crossly she dragged her mind back from Sally and that particular thing about her which more experienced persons could have told Cerise was nothing more nor less than *allure*. No woman in Cerise's family had ever had it, yet, Cerise had to remind herself, there had been some very sensible and even happy marriages in her family. Until the day when some man should decide that Cerise (in spite of her unusual and ridiculously glamorous name) would make him a good sensible wife, she told herself, there was work to be done.

She sat down and got on with it, with that dogged application that drove Sally Marston up the wall, as she herself would have put it. Sally's irritation at Cerise's ability to concentrate anywhere and under any circumstances rose each day, but Cerise was unaware of it. She still liked Sally very much, and had accepted the fact that they would always be firm friends.

She wrote as much to her favourite aunt (whose turn it was to hear from her) as soon as she had finished her written work. 'Sally is a thoroughly nice girl, but shockingly misunderstood,' she said firmly, and never paused to give a thought to what that statement would mean to her aunt when she read it. Cerise had no imagination, but she understood the meaning of the word duty, and as soon as she had finished chatting in the letter about her life at the hospital, she faithfully recorded for her aunt's interest all the things they had tackled that day in class; the bile and pancreas, the evils of contamination of water, the sewage farm system and the salivary glands. She also said that they were to visit a farm in the district within the next day or so, and that her drawing of the nervous system had pleased Sister Tutor.

Sally was recounting the same ground, but with less accuracy and far more colour, for the benefit of Dr Bruce Carmichael, over tea consisting of cream buns of five different kinds, and tea with cream in it. He stirred his tea, which he took with lemon instead of milk, and ate dry toast, which seemed to Sally disgusting. Tea was a meal that saved one from getting irritable in the arid length of hours between lunch and the evening meal. It was sacrilege not to make the most of it.

'I've undertaken to become a nurse and I'm putting a great deal of energy and strength into it,' she told him quite seriously, 'but I didn't see the use of going to see the loathsome state of old man Jones's land, on which he usually dumps the contents of his privy. He has no main drainage, they say, and the exercise is to go there first and then to Potts' Manor which is so modern that even the cows aren't allowed to roll in the muck.'

Bruce winced, but his mouth twitched. Sally had always amused him – that was to say when she wasn't concentrating on fighting him.

'We also had to do the bile and pancreas, which I think is frankly insulting, considering we did that years ago at school, so I thought I'd get on to my nervous system. Well, frankly, anyone who says they recognise one nerve from another is just a fool. I couldn't see any difference. I remembered an aerial photograph of the railway lines at Crewe, so I just drew in similar lines on my blank body, and Sister Tut came up behind me and said it was a creditable attempt! Well, I ask you! Poor old patients, when I get weaving among them!'

'Never mind, you'll be rumbled long before then,' Bruce Carmichael told her, rather grimly.

'Oh, no, I shan't. You don't know what I'm capable of. I'm absolutely determined to qualify, if only to show you and that Roberta how wrong you can both be.'

He suddenly went very still, and his jaw was even grimmer than before. Sally wondered for one awful moment whether she had gone too far. Now she knew Matron by sight having almost cannoned into her in the yard as she crossed to X-ray a long way behind the rest of her set, having stopped to tie up her shoe-lace, Sally felt that she could now understand the family connection between Bruce and Miss York. The jawline was exactly the same, and so was the warning glint in the eye. She had just a trace more respect for Bruce, for a fleeting moment.

'Why do you connect me with Roberta?' he asked in a deceptively mild voice.

Sally shrugged. This, she felt, was one of his best 'lunatic' questions, not to be treated seriously. In a cussed mood, she embarked on treating it seriously, just to show him.

'Why not? Your minds both move on the same lines – I can tell that, because anything you say to me sounds just like Roberta talking, allowing for the difference in the voice. A sort of lecturing way of telling me some information I want – I noticed it particularly when you told me at the start of this quite decent spread about the quick sale of our old house and the condition of Mummy's legs.'

'Thank you very much,' he said sarcastically. 'What else.'

'Oh, she's always saying what a wonderful man you are, and what a marvellous doctor, and you're always saying what a marvellous nurse he is, and what a good wife she'll make some man. Mutual admiration society. I wish you both future joy together, in advance.'

He watched her warily. Now for it, she told herself. In colloquial language, I'm about to get torn off a jolly big strip, and serve me right for opening my big mouth so wide.

But that didn't happen. Bruce said mildly, 'Perhaps Roberta never favoured you with her confidence. She happens to be in love with someone else, and much as I admire her, I doubt if I would want to marry her. She knows that.'

Far from helping, that little speech of his made matters very much worse, because into Sally's mind leapt the thought: That's it, Roberta's too keen on my father!

He watched Sally's face diffuse with dark angry colour, and he wondered what could possibly be in his words to make her like that. He gave it up. Sally could force him to feel far too many stormy emotions in one hour than was good for his blood pressure.

'Do you honestly like it at the hospital?' he asked her.

She considered the point, caught off guard. Not for worlds would she admit that she had had a bad fright the other night when the R.M.O. caught her in such an invidious position and she had thought she would be asked to leave. Not for anything was she going to let Bruce Carmichael know she was beginning to enjoy the life, and to feel as if she might soon 'belong' somewhere. 'It's not so ghastly as I expected it to be, but I might find I'm wrong later,' was all she would say.

'But you're going to stick it out, to spite me.'

'That's right,' she told him, with a cheerful grin.

'No use asking why you dislike me, I suppose?'

'That's one of your best daft questions, isn't it, Dr Carmichael, since you know I'm not sufficiently bothered to rise to the heights of disliking … anyone.'

His face flamed at that, and whitened.

'I apologise if I sounded ill-mannered,' she said quickly, stiffly. Then, indignation flaring at the apparent injustice, she stormed at him: 'You lay little traps for me, don't you? Just to make me flop into them, flat on my face, and then you can sit there looking all righteous, knowing I have to apologise! It isn't fair!'

'You could avoid it by being reasonable and not falling over backwards to do the exact opposite to what you think I want you to do,' he said coldly, striving to tamp down the rising anger at her words.

'My mother always told me to meet bad manners with good, only she never explained how that could be done,' Sally added. 'Also she told me that I'd always be meeting someone who rubbed my back up the wrong way, and then she went out of her way to provide someone who'd always be popping in and out of the house, with just that quality – you!'

'Perhaps this tea might be terminated now,' he said quietly, 'before we say something we might be sorry for. I'd like to formally apologise for anything you think I've done to annoy you. I assure you I didn't intend to.'

'You sound as if you're thinking that you can't be bothered about me enough to try to annoy me,' she said, under her breath.

'Perhaps I did,' he heard himself retorting, to his horror. And this was how it always was. He started out feeling tender and amused, and then the situation deteriorated down the scale until he wanted to shake her until she stopped annoying him.

He looked at her in despair as she got up from the table and swept her handbag off it, to go across the restaurant, head in air, to the ladies' room to make up her face.

What had he done, to make the conversation such a shambles? He was certain it was his fault, somehow, because she had started off in a rather cheerful, gay mood – for Sally, that was. She usually acted pretty glum when she was forced to be with him for more than a few minutes. There had been happiness … no, that wasn't quite right. Satisfaction, perhaps, under her manner. He had begun to think she really liked being a student nurse.

From then onwards he had meant to work the conversation around to tackling her as to what had happened at that job at the hotel, which she had left so quickly. He had been given a brief account of her fright over the horse which had terminated the job at the riding school, but no reason at all for her leaving the receptionist job that one of his patients had got for her. He meant to have that reason, but he had missed his chance today, somehow.

He sighed, and signalled to the waitress to give him the bill, then Sally came back.

She had cooled down a bit, so he ventured

to ask her when she expected her next full day off, but she forestalled him.

'Don't you think,' she said, in a cool little voice that made him forget his prepared speech in sheer surprise, 'that as we obviously can't conduct a conversation together in a civilised manner, we might as well call off this sort of thing? It's kind of you (the intention, I mean) to come and visit me, but it really isn't necessary. I have plenty to do in my free time, and as you reminded me from the first, there's plenty of opportunity to make friends of my own age group.'

This, too, caught him on the wrong foot. She made him feel so very much her senior in that moment.

'Besides, you're being so kind already in looking after my parents. I should be a lot happier if you forgot about me–'

'I can't do that, Sally,' he put in swiftly, but she misunderstood.

'Oh, go on, of course you can! Do you mean to tell me you visit the daughter of every patient of yours who happens to be away getting well? And the letters, too – you must be sick of writing, after you're through a day's work. Let's call those off, too, shall we?'

CHAPTER SIX

It was during the week that followed that a very disturbed letter came to Sally from her mother. She wasn't to know it, but Mrs Marston knew that her next operation was coming up, and neither she nor the doctors were very happy about it. She particularly didn't want Sally to know this; not because she thought Sally might worry, so much as that Sally might write a separate letter to her father and mention it. Sally's father was in a different hospital, and it felt to her mother as if he were half a world away.

'I pin my faith,' she wrote to Sally, 'on Bruce Carmichael. He is a wonderful person. He has promised to keep us all in touch with each other – your father, you and me – and I do hope that you will feel free to go to him with any little troubles you may have, my dear.'

Sally frowned. She wasn't unduly sensitive, but this sounded like a letter before a person is going away for a long journey or setting out to do something dangerous and isn't expecting to come back.

Cerise watched her anxiously, every time she put her book down to memorise her list of surgical instruments. With Sally looking so tense, like a coiled spring, over this letter, it wasn't easy to concentrate. Sally usually skimmed a letter, put it down for closer perusal later, and lost it. Cerise was always retrieving mislaid letters from under the bureau or in pockets of garments thrown out for the laundry.

She said to Sally, 'Is something wrong, Marston?'

Sally shrugged irritably. 'I don't know. A most peculiar letter from Mummy. One of those letters you're supposed to read between the lines, and I'm not good at it. So far as I can see, it's a "be-nice-to-dear-Dr-Carmichael" effort, but I don't see why I should be. He annoys me. Besides–'

'Besides what?'

'Oh, I don't know. I thought – I kept thinking – that he was keen on Roberta. I told you, didn't I?'

'Your mother's nurse,' Cerise agreed, catching up on the information she had had from Sally so far. 'And isn't he?'

'He quite definitely and categorically told me he wasn't, that Roberta was keen on someone else, and that she wasn't the one he would want to marry anyway.'

'Well, that's good, isn't it? I mean, you did say you wouldn't want her to be the wife of your own doctor, as I remember it?'

'I know, but then he said she was keen on someone else, and who do you suppose that's likely to be?'

Cerise, listening to the fierce tones in Sally's voice, remembered with a sense of shock that Sally had been so sure at one time that Roberta was getting too fond of Sally's father.

'Oh, no, I can't think she'd be fond of your father, knowingly,' Cerise put in quickly. 'It wouldn't be ethical, and she does sound a very good nurse. Straight and all that.'

'Oh, does she!'

Sally got up and started pacing up and down, reducing the small room to the size of a cage in the zoo. Cerise felt Sally was really a tiger at this moment, and that if the absent Roberta were here, Sally would pounce on her. How could someone nice like Sally dislike someone like that efficient nurse so much?

'I don't think I quite understand why Roberta is staying on,' Cerise said gently. 'After all, if your mother and father are going to have treatment at hospitals in Switzerland–'

'Here, read my mother's letter and see what you make of it,' Sally said unexpectedly, and dropped it into Cerise's lap.

Cerise hesitated, then opened it out. After the exceedingly uncertain opening paragraph, Mrs Marston went on, 'I want to feel you are happy in your new job, but more than that, I want to feel you are *settled.* I sometimes think, lying here, that it must be awful for you to know we are so far away and home sold up, but I didn't know what else we could have done. I think, too, that it might have helped if I could have seen you working in those two jobs you left so precipitately, but of course, that was never possible. If only I could have got as far as your school that day, and talked with the staff, I might have divined what it was about that excellent establishment that was making you sound so restless and miserable and *trapped.*'

'Did you feel trapped?' Cerise asked, looking up suddenly. 'At your school, I mean?'

'Never mind that,' Sally said briskly. 'Read on!'

Cerise read on. 'I don't think I'd worry about any of this now, if it wasn't for what Roberta said the other day. I don't think she realised she said it, and I didn't say anything to her about it afterwards. It was one of those odd little remarks dropped, that make one think on a new line. I have waited for her to amplify it since, or to say something else that would assure me that I have been imagining things, but she hasn't. And so I must ask you, my dear, and pray that you will tell me, if only to set my mind at rest: was the man you were interested in free?'

Cerise's head shot up and the two girls looked at each other. 'Read on!' Sally said, tight-lipped.

Cerise did, and the rest of the letter didn't sound as bad as that last sentence had suggested it might be. But Cerise saw Sally's point: her mother worried around a thought until almost accidentally she might get something out of it.

'By *free,* I mean, someone old enough to offer a young girl something, and not just a lad tied down to his studies, perhaps at university, still on the bounty of his parents. That is what I thought might have been the case at your school – you still having to finish your studies and the boy you loved miles away finishing his, and life seeming to be galloping by and everything perfectly futile. And when you came home, you were a whole year at home and I could never really understand what had happened. I know there was someone you cared for specially, because sometimes you had that impatient look in your face, and the trapped look in your eyes, as if the four walls of home couldn't hold you.'

Cerise said, 'Your mother isn't as out of touch as you seem to think, is she, Marston?'

'She's way off the beam,' said Sally, between her teeth. 'Read on! You really ought to plough all through it, to get the real picture.'

So Cerise finished what was by now becoming rather a personal letter, although Sally didn't seem to regard it as such.

'I did try to talk to you, but you just dried up, Sally, my dear, but I'm so far away and so worried about you, and although I don't expect I shall ever be told what happened at the riding school or the hotel, I would like to know what happened at your school. I do earnestly beg of you to try and tell our dear doctor, even if you can't bring yourself to tell your own mother.'

'Well?' Sally asked impatiently, as Cerise folded the letter and returned it to her, with heightened colour. 'What do you think?'

'It seems to me that your mother guesses what happened. Would that be possible?' Cerise said at last.

'She guesses there was man. So what? You know there was, Oldham. I'm seeing him now, aren't I?' Sally fumed. 'But what I don't like about it is she doesn't say just what dear Roberta dropped by way of that loaded remark. Roberta's good at dropping a remark that sets everything in a turmoil. Mummy calls it "making people think for themselves", but I call it diabolical and sheer nosiness. I would, at times, dearly like to strangle Roberta. I wish our dear doctor would marry her. She'd lead him a dance!'

'If I were your mother, Marston, I'd be worried sick, too,' Cerise said quietly.

'Why? Do you think I can't look after myself?'

'Marston, you're the same age as me, so I know what it feels like. Oh, I know I've never had a man-friend, but I've had problems, and to me they seemed pretty big, at times. The thing is, at our age, sometimes one gets a sinking feeling as if the world were too big and unfriendly. I know one hates to admit it. I doubt if I'd tell anyone else except you. But you see, I do understand.'

'So?' Sally stormed.

'I'm too used to you by now to mind you looking at me as if I'd turned into your Roberta,' Cerise smiled. 'No, what I'm thinking is, you've told me a certain amount, and I've tried to fill in the gaps. It seems to be that you've been in pretty deep water this last year, but you've managed to pull out. Well, almost, only you're scared stiff that the things that have happened are past but won't lie down. That's the most awful thing to have – the feeling of being scared to look over your shoulder, I should think!'

'Am I as obvious as that?' Sally gasped.

'No. Perhaps I'm as nosey as your Roberta. Or perhaps it's just because we room together and we get to know each other pretty well. I don't know. But it does seem to me that you get nightmares about it.'

'Do I talk in my sleep?' Sally demanded.

'You shout out sometimes, but it's unintelligible. I get the feeling that you're anxious about something – perhaps about your parents. That would be natural.'

'I'm not worried about them,' said Sally, in surprise. 'Whatever else I might feel about Dr Carmichael, I do trust him to know his job as a doctor, and if he says he knows a man who can do something for my parents, then I believe him. He'd better not let me down!' she added darkly, which brought a smile to Cerise's lips.

'Then it must be that something pretty

awful happened to you in this past year, and you've only just got out of it by the skin of your teeth. Am I right?'

Sally didn't answer, but her very silence was as good as admitting that Cerise was right.

'I'm not asking you to tell me about it,' Cerise said quietly. 'Why I mentioned it at all was that it did occur to me that this Roberta had thought on the same lines and guessed, because she might well have other information to go on. Well, she does know the people you worked with and I don't. And living in the district she might have heard someone talking, and of course, I wouldn't have that advantage. It isn't difficult to put two and two together about someone in trouble, if you study them and have some of the facts. But you see, she might think your parents ought to know, for your good, and that's her way of dropping a hint, so they'll guess the rest.'

Sally looked really anxious now. 'I don't do bad things,' she said, in a low intense voice, 'if that's what you're thinking. But I will admit that bad things happen to me, simply because I have the most appalling bad luck. I don't suppose anyone in our set could have had the things happen to them that I have had, simply because I'm me. Stick my neck out, and *wham!* – there I am, deep in the muck. Well, I've got out of it, and I'm going to stay out, but I am not going to talk about it, not to my parents or our dear doctor or anyone. Sorry, Oldham, nothing against you, but the fact is, if I talk about it it will bring it all back, and that's not a good thing, to my way of thinking.'

'You know best,' Cerise said quietly. 'If you let the past act as a lesson to steer clear of things in the future, then that's all right. By the way, is your mother expecting that operation soon?'

Sally's head shot up. 'No, I don't think so. She doesn't say so, does she? Well, you know me – I might have skimmed through too quickly and missed it.'

'No, she doesn't say so,' Cerise assured Sally.

'Then that's all right,' Sally said, and put the letter away. 'Parents! Why can't they leave one alone?'

But she did sit down and write to her mother, within the next half hour, Cerise noticed.

She found Cerise looking at her thoughtfully, so she offered the information: 'I've written and told Mummy that the fellow I was keen on was certainly free, so she isn't to worry on that score, but much water under the bridge since then.'

'Is that true?' Cerise seemed to be genuinely surprised.

Sally turned sharply away. 'Yes, it's true. You're a pest, Oldham – you drag the truth from me, don't you? Every time! All right, the big heart-throb has swooped into my life again, reduced me to a miserable quaking jelly, and faded out again. At least, he let me down the last time, so – there you are! I'm the world's worst mug. Uncle, indeed! Wouldn't you think I'd learn a lesson from the way he acts and let him go? Don't get bitten by the bug I've been bitten by, Oldham. It's hell, I can assure you, and there's no future in it.'

'It's not as bad as being keen on someone who hasn't realised you're alive and polluting the earth,' Cerise said wryly. 'At least you do have him to yourself sometimes, and presumably you get something out of it to dream over when you're alone. Which is something, believe me!'

Sally looked curiously at her friend. Such an attitude staggered her. She had never been short of admiring men and boys in her young life. Even at day school she could always be sure of some doting little boy who would carry her satchel for her. How could someone as nice as Cerise never have had a man in her life? That defeated Sally.

'Oh, well, we're a couple of mutts. We've got our health and strength, and what's a man or two here and there? I suppose I shall fall heavily for someone else, a little later on. Someone to blot Frank out,' she said, half under her breath. That was the first time she had mentioned his christian name to Cerise, and the way she said it stabbed at Cerise. Knowing Sally, she was surprised that anyone could dig so deeply into Sally's consciousness, and having done so, Cerise didn't think Sally would find it so easy to replace him by some other man. Not to quite the same extent.

'We'd better get back to our work, anyway,' Cerise agreed quietly. 'Finish your letter and I'll hear your notes if you like.'

'Haven't done them,' Sally said cheerfully. 'How shall I finish this flipping letter to Mummy? Oh, yes, I'll tell her about the visit to the farm tomorrow. Of all the mad things to have to do, visit a farm. I think I've told her about it in a previous letter, haven't I? Yes, I'm sure I have. Then I know what I'll tell her!'

And she wrote: 'I room with a girl called

Cerise Oldham, who looks after me, although she is only the same age as me, so you don't have to worry. She's sensible and very sweet and comes from a long line of nurses, midwives, doctors, and hospital personnel. In fact, she has to do a duty letter to each of the relatives in turn, to tell them what she's been learning, so they can keep tabs on her. So you see, I'm in very good hands, and you don't need to worry. Our time out is restricted, and Dr Carmichael comes and does duty visits every so often and asks me searching questions. There is, I assure you, very little scope for being a nuisance to anyone,' and then she sent her love and closed the letter.

'Here, Oldham, read this!' she said, shooting it across the room so that it skimmed, as usual, under the chest.

Cerise fished it out and read it. It grieved her that Sally shouldn't feel her letters to her own mother were too personal for other people's eyes, and yet she was flattered that Sally should confide in her even to that extent.

'You shouldn't have done that!' she said sharply.

'It's true. You are all the things I've said!'

'Yes, be that as it may be (which I doubt) it also puts a certain amount of responsibility on my shoulders, and it isn't true that there isn't much scope for you to be a nuisance to anyone. You know that, Marston!'

'Well, never mind. Forget it. Tell me instead something I badly want to hear – why do we have to go to this wretched farm?'

'Two farms, Marston, and you know why. You're just changing the subject. We've to compare the two, and anyway, it *is* important.'

'How? I mean, I can understand having to learn how to make beds and bed-bath people, and do all the drudgery bits of nursing, and the first aid, and learning the instruments so one doesn't give the surgeon the wrong one in theatre and all that, by a mistake (which I'm sure I would make!) but why visit farms? Can't we safely leave that to the authorities to see the thing is hygienic?'

'My aunt, who was a ward sister, was telling us once that a patient came in with an absolutely unknown bug. She had been visiting relatives on a farm. My aunt had visited a farm once, that was small and not very organised, and it gave her the clue to the diagnosis – a bug from the manure pile because it was too near the house.'

'Well, that's not very new, is it? Anyway, why does a nurse have to know? Don't the doctors do the diagnosis?'

'Don't sound so alarmed, Marston! You don't have to be the sort of nurse who is good at diagnosis, but some nurses are born like that, and the medical and surgical staff think a lot of them.'

'I bet they do; anything to get someone else to do their work. That's men for you! Well, I'm not going to!'

'Oh, I don't know – to me, that's half the interest of the job. Almost like being an amateur detective. Well, it's much more fun, surely, to weigh up all the symptoms and have a smack at diagnosing, mentally I mean, and then offering your findings if you get asked!'

'*If* you're asked!' Sally said in disgust.

'Yes, well, in the R.M.O.'s lecture last night–' Cerise began, then turned sharply away, her cheeks pink, as she caught Sally's eye.

There was a moment's uncomfortable silence, then Sally said, with a wide yawn, 'Oh, let's get on with these notes. You can ask me if you like, but I shan't know a single right answer. Roll on tomorrow, and the pigs and cows!'

The next day was a drizzling one. A cold little wind took over when the rain did stop, and then there was a wind and the rain too. The girls unenthusiastically marched round the small farm and held their noses and did their best to disentangle the heavy brogue from the farmer's comments, and make something of the visit. The modern farm was different. The bus, having taken them there, left them under cover, and the clean light painted walls and thick glass, the milking machinery and the sterile cleanliness everywhere reminded them of a modern factory as much as anything. It wasn't easy to decide which was the farmer here either, and they later discovered that this farm was run by five brothers and a very large staff.

It was when they were leaving the milking section that it happened: that first flick of the past, to remind Sally that it wasn't true what she had said to Cerise about having put it all behind her. It was there, very much so, and she felt considerably jolted.

Even on this modern farm, the land itself was still as muddy as any other farm land in this sort of weather, and as the girls walked across to the bus that was waiting to take them back, a group of young riders came in, in charge of a rather hard-faced girl with a leather jacket and a head-square instead of the hard hat the others were wearing.

Recognition struggled with incredulity, and Sally was left standing there, as the others went towards the bus. But as the riders went by, they shot up a shower of mud, and Sally caught the lot.

They wheeled back, and apologised: five children between the ages of nine and fifteen. It was perfunctory apology, it was true, and they soon cantered off, but that girl with them merely smiled faintly, and said nothing.

Iris Leame. Her name suddenly came back to Sally, from the distance of six months ago, and clicked into place, although Sally found it hard at first to believe she was here. But then, of course, she had probably come across country from the riding school to coach these children – all sons and daughters of the five brothers who ran the farm. It was incredible that this should be so. Surely they would have been taken to the riding school and brought back!

Later Sally heard the explanation: Iris Leame was related to neighbours of this farm, and it was quite natural that she should be here doing this sort of thing.

'What do you find so extraordinary about it?' Cerise asked blankly, after Sally had furiously told her several times that she couldn't believe it, that that girl of all people should be here today.

'She was the one who caused me to get kicked out of the riding school,' Sally explained, with set lips.

'Well, I shouldn't worry,' Cerise said at last. 'I suppose it goes a lot deeper than a lost job, but you're not likely to tell me what it is! I suppose if the facts were known, she lost her boy-friend to you!'

Cerise said it in a half joking way, trying to turn Sally's mind from the incident, but Sally's chin jerked up and she stared stormily into Cerise's face, and Cerise knew that her idiotic remark had struck near the truth.

'Well, if it *is* the case, my dear, it's a thing you'll have to learn to live with, won't you?' Cerise protested, and she thought of the R.M.O. and the times he managed to walk past the Nurses Home since the occasion when he had taken Sally out. She sighed. 'Anyway, what does it matter? She's out of your life, now, isn't she? It's bad luck you ran into her today, but unless she breaks her leg and comes into hospital the first day you go on the wards, how can she bother you?'

'Don't laugh! Don't say things like that, either, Oldham! I'm not superstitious. I just don't like saying things like that, in case Fate hears and they happen to come true!'

She said as much to Bruce Carmichael when he suddenly turned up on her full day off. She didn't ask herself why he had come: she just pounced on him to ask him what was bothering her mother, to write such a letter.

Bruce looked guarded. 'When did you get this letter, Sally?' he asked her carefully.

He had taken her to Queenswood for lunch, and there was a rather nice park with botanical gardens and a length of the river emptying itself into a huge lake. They stood on the bridge watching small boats going underneath, and a swan making its stately way along the edge. Sally took her time in answering. She wasn't slow to notice his wariness.

Finally she rummaged in her handbag and gave it to him. 'See the date yourself. Read the whole thing, and what she says about you, too. What am I supposed to confide in you?'

He read the letter. 'It seems to me that your mother thinks there's something worrying you,' he said at last. 'She hasn't seen you as recently as I have, and I myself would say that there was something that had upset you since my last visit. Would I be right?'

She shrugged irritably. 'Oh, yes, I suppose so. I don't like going back to places and things. And I don't like people I've met, and left behind in the past, to suddenly pop up again.' All except Frank, her heart clamoured. *All except Frank.*

'Who has popped up again? Come on, you'd better tell me all about it, Sally.'

She stared stormily down at the lake. 'A girl who taught the kids to ride, at the riding school. Name of Iris Leame.'

The sullenness in her tones made him wonder. 'Go on. Your best enemy, I suppose?'

'You can say that again! All right,' she said, between her teeth. 'I was bored, bored, bored! Mucking out the stables, when I could have been teaching the kids. I'm a good horsewoman, aren't I? I'd have made a better job at teaching them than she did!'

'Oh, so that's it!' he said softly. 'And what about the horse that frightened you? Speaking personally, I have yet to see the horse that could do that. I would say it might be the other way round.'

'Very funny,' she said bitterly. 'There did happen to be such a horse – a rogue horse. Perhaps you haven't met one,' she finished with exaggerated kindness.

'I've met one. I've been kicked by one. But I doubt if I'd go running home to tell them I couldn't keep on in that job because of it.'

'And neither did I,' she too him up swiftly. Then she realised what she had let out, and she bit her lip hard.

'Well, having said so much, what do you propose to do about it now?' he asked, his face crinkling up into an amused grin.

'I could kill you!' she said under her breath. 'All right, this is what happened, but I'd be glad if you didn't tell my parents. It was ... oh, not nice.'

He frowned, but he didn't interrupt her, as she began, 'There was a man – name of Quentin Farrell.'

Bruce Carmichael's face cleared. He thought he could see what the trouble was. Someone making a pass at Sally and she lost her temper, chastised him and walked out.

But it wasn't as simple as that, it seemed. 'I neither liked nor disliked him,' Sally went on slowly, throwing leaves down into the water, that she had been tearing off a nearby bush, without noticing what she was doing. 'He was a bit of a bore when it came to waylaying me to talk. It did occur to me that there might be trouble if it got to the boss's ears, though even that was doubtful. Did you know the boss of the riding school? A queer sort of man, didn't say much. Captain Philpotts. Don't ask me what he was a captain of. But he had a wife who was much younger than he was and really quite awfully good-looking. He followed her with his eyes all the time, as if he was afraid of letting her out of his sight, and she made it quite plain that she was bored stiff with him.'

'Go on,' Bruce encouraged.

'Oh, well, I was fool enough to try and see him to ask if I could be promoted from mucking out the stables, but all I got was good old stalwart Quentin Farrell. You know, he was the big husky type, supposed to be in charge of the riding programmes and the stables, but actually to keep pests like me away from the boss.'

Sally smiled, rather grimly. 'Still, he said he'd see what he could do, with that sort of be-nice-to-me look, and I was going to tell him what I thought of him, only … well, I didn't.'

'Why not?' he asked her gently.

'Well, if you must know, there had been someone I was frightfully keen on and I thought he liked me quite a bit,' she said in a muffled voice, turning her head away, 'only I found out I was wrong, and he let me down. In point of fact, it was while I was supposed to be meeting him that I got held up and late for getting back to school, and I was thrown out on my ear. Surprised? The parents don't keep you briefed because they didn't know about it.'

Now he looked angry, but not for the reason she thought. He was wildly, unreasoningly angry to think there had been some other man in her life, so early, and who had trifled with her affections.

Sally went on, 'Well, I was doing my best to be sensible and *get over* him, so I thought, well, it's time dear Quentin was useful to me, so I let him ... console me. In a platonic way – well, almost. Not much romantic love because quite frankly although he thought he was a whale of a fellow he really hadn't a clue how to go about being romantic. He just followed me around looking pretty silly, and he escorted me off the premises at night and things like that, and ... well,' she finished, suddenly losing patience with the whole thing, 'to cut a long, long story short, he was the man Iris Leame was keen on, she saw him following me around and she felt like mayhem. She set the rogue horse at me.'

That took Bruce Carmichael aback so much, just by the sudden way she terminated that hesitant narrative, that he got the wrong idea. 'But that was dangerous! Why didn't you tell someone? Goodness, we could have taken proceedings!'

'Dear, dear Dr Carmichael, you still haven't got the picture,' Sally said, exasperated. 'All right, perhaps I'm not telling it very well. That, I meant, was what she planned to do – send me out on the rogue horse to exercise it. It was the sort of brute who trotted quietly, then suddenly tossed its rider. I didn't know that, but in point of fact, I wasn't the one who went on it.'

'Explain, and very slowly, Sally,' he said grimly.

'Iris wouldn't let herself be seen near him, of course, so she told the stable boy (who was new) to collect the rider in the anorak with the red and blue patterns all over it – my anorak, in short!'

'So you–' he began, but she shook her head.

'No, no, no, not me, because it was a mouldy cold day and I'd lent my anorak to some other girl who'd joined that week. I was warm enough, and inside, anyway. So she went, she was thrown, and – well, she got it pretty badly. Internal injuries as well, and to crown it all, she was a great friend of Iris.'

'Good grief! Sally, why didn't you *tell* me–'

'Because I could never get you alone, and anyway you would have told all the others,' she said fiercely. 'Anyway, Iris was so hopping mad that she just had to hit back, so she thought up something else, only I never really worked out what. I think she sent me on a message to the boss's study for some special reason, only I think something went wrong. Some people were in the room, talking in a low tone, and I knocked and went in, and the far door was just shutting – I never found out who had been there. But the boss came in and he was furious to find me there, and later there was an awful carry-on because one of his beastly trophies was missing.'

White-faced, she glared at Bruce. 'He thought *I'd* taken it!' she said indignantly. 'Well, when he wouldn't believe me, I just walked out. I was so furious, I could have kicked anyone within sight. Oh, yes, I know I should have told someone at home about it, but what would you have said if I had? Mummy in that state from her accident, and Daddy pretty sick and dear Roberta clinging so I could never get anyone alone to talk about things private and personal!'

'Why didn't you confide in Roberta?' he asked mildly.

'Are you serious?' she asked him scornfully. 'You really don't like her, do you?'

He looked so much as if he *did* like Roberta

that it ruined the giving of confidences. She was finished, then, and when he said, 'Well now, we come to what I really want to know – what happened about the hotel receptionist job that one of my patients got for you?' she just shrugged and turned away.

'Sally! I'm asking you – what happened, for you to lose it so quickly?'

'Haven't a clue! Probably my late boss warned them to lock up the silver when I was around!' and the hurt in her young face convinced him that this was perhaps the case. And yet he couldn't help feeling that there was an awful lot that she had omitted to tell him.

CHAPTER SEVEN

Although Sally wouldn't have admitted it to anyone else, she had to admit to herself that meeting Iris Leame at the farm had given her a nasty jolt. She kept thinking of the way that Iris had looked at her in that first startled moment of recognition on both sides. Iris would have recognised the uniform Sally was wearing, of course, and now it was likely that she would run into Sally again.

Sally took herself to task sharply over that aspect of it. What could Iris hope to do, even if she did now know how to find Sally? Surely Iris had done enough, one way or another? She couldn't possibly want to go on hounding Sally out of every job she took, surely? And then, too, Sally told herself, it was a bit stupid to think it was Iris who was hounding her out of jobs. The one at the riding school? Perhaps. Iris had been rather bitter over her friend getting so badly hurt, although it had been, of course, the fault of Iris from the start. But beyond that? Had it been Iris who had caused Captain Philpotts to go to his study close on Sally's heels, or had he had a natural reason for needing to go to his study? And who had been there before? Who had gone so quietly out of that far door, the moment Sally knocked and walked in?

Come to think of it, they must have slipped out when they heard her footsteps in the passage, because after she had knocked, she had, by force of habit, waited a moment before going in, and in that momentary pause the room beyond had seemed to be still, unnaturally still, empty.

Something teased her about all this. Iris had been most particular about Sally taking that message over then, at once – and yet, at the time, Sally had felt that there hadn't been much of importance about the message to merit such haste. It was, looking back, almost as if Iris had wanted her to be there in that study.

Remembering the dislike that had been in Iris's eyes even in that brief moment at the farm the other day, Sally suddenly realised that Iris might well have hidden the trophy to make it seem that Sally had taken it. She must have banked on Captain Philpotts not descending to the level of having Sally searched – or perhaps she had suggested that Sally had got rid of it to someone else. Sally didn't know. She only knew that the riding school hadn't been a happy place: filled with rumours. Rumours of the boss's wife not being faithful to him, rumours of this or that person about to be sacked, rumours of things being stolen. The lot.

As she thought about it, staring into space when she ought to have been copying the graph from the blackboard of the infectious disease level in this country in the last twenty-five years, Sally thought about that empty room again, and the murmuring of those two voices just before the room had become empty. A man's voice, she recalled, and a woman's ... and then she realised what it was all about.

She heard Sister Tutor saying sarcastically to the class, 'And I am sure that Nurse Marston can tell us all, in the twinkling of an eye, the exact number. She knows it so well that she doesn't even have to look at the graph – she can afford to stare into the middle distance and relax.'

Sally brought herself back with an effort. Cerise was looking at her in an agonised way, mouthing the answer to help Sally out.

Sally suddenly hadn't patience with any of it. The awful realisation of what she had been grappling to find out for so many months suddenly sickened her. She didn't want people, she didn't want a job, she just wanted to get away from everything, to somewhere where it was clean, no intrigues – no deceit or plotting, nothing to fear.

'Might I be excused?' she stuttered, stumbling to her feet. 'I actually feel rather dreadful.'

Cerise half rose in her seat, and the sarcastic smile left Sister Tutor's face, as Sally swayed a little, and stumbled to the door without waiting for permission.

'Shall I go with her, Sister?' Cerise asked, on a gasping note. 'She's a peculiar colour, isn't she?'

'No, I'm all right,' Sally said fiercely from the door, and closed it firmly behind her. But she hadn't gone very far before she ran full tilt into the arms of Home Sister, and there was Sister Tutor coming briskly along the corridor, with a short, pithy explanation. Sally was promptly taken to the sick bay.

The R.M.O. came up presently to have a look at her. He and Home Sister decided she had got a 'bug' and must be kept there for two or three days.

He came back, after Home Sister had left him. The door was left circumspectly open, but he stood there looking at Sally for a few minutes, that half amused smile playing round his mouth.

'Why,' he asked softly, 'did you appear so surprised to find you *had* a roaring temperature?'

'You think I was faking being sick, didn't you?' she said fiercely. 'Well, I was. I just had to get out of that classroom, to think. I really couldn't care less about that stupid graph on the blackboard. Does that shock you, sir?'

'Let's say it staggers me that anyone can give the impression, at your age, of being interested in it at all,' he remarked, still amused.

It flabbergasted her. It was heresy for him to say such a thing, and her look betrayed her thoughts.

'Let's say I'm rather an unconventional R.M.O.,' he said gravely. 'I have the uncomfortable habit of speaking my thoughts aloud. As a point of fact, some of the best nurses we have flunked lessons to a certain extent in P.T.S. and let it be known that they weren't wildly enthusiastic about the written work at times. Not to worry. But what about answering my question more fully?'

'I'd just had a shock, but I didn't think that could make one feel quite so awful inside.'

'Well, it's been a useful lesson this morning after all, then, if you've learned how the poor old patient feels on receiving a shock,' he remarked. 'Any use asking how you experienced such a thing, in the safe confines of a P.T.S. classroom?'

She shrugged. 'Remembering that awful last year of mine. Something that had puzzled me suddenly clicked into place. It wasn't nice.'

'And?' he prompted gently.

'And I remembered some horrible Shakespeare thing we had to learn at school. Some ghastly character suddenly realises his friends have been ganging up against him pretty cunningly and successfully, and he looks as if he's eaten some bad food and raves about plotting most foul, or something. I don't know – I can't remember the words. At the time I know I thought he was making a great fuss about nothing, but now I think I understand how he felt. I mean, the people you have around you – you might not necessarily like them or think they like you, but to suddenly realise that certain things they've being doing mean they are actually planning to do you real harm – *ugh!* It's a quite horrid feeling!'

Her eyes were round with the appalled realisation still fresh in her. He stared down at her, considering. 'Of course, I appreciate how you feel, but it might help if you could give me the actual details.'

'Oh, why not? There was a man who was supposed to be the property of some stupid girl I worked with at the riding school, and the clot decided he liked me and she got peeved and sent me on a message. I couldn't think why. It was a jolly silly message. But now I believe I was supposed to break in on the boss's wife having a petting party with a friend of hers.' Distaste riddled Sally's clean young face.

'Nice people!' the R.M.O. commented.

'Did your parents know about this?'

'No! How could I let them? My mother was injured in an accident on the train coming to see me at my school – she can't walk any more. And my father collapsed through worry about her. How could I tell them?'

'So you fought the battle on your own,' he said, still in that soft, warm voice.

He hadn't somehow given her the chance to go on to tell him about Captain Philpotts turning up not long afterwards, and the incident of the missing trophy. Oh, well, what did it matter? Sally asked herself tiredly.

'I'll have something written up to make you sleep,' the R.M.O. promised.

That old thing, Sally thought. She had already heard the first-years discussing this panacea for most ills. But all the same, she was very glad to feel the blessed sensation of slipping away, slipping away from all her troubles.

She heard (or thought she heard) the R.M.O. murmur something about wanting to hear more about that job of hers, when she was well again.

The rest did her good. After two days she was about again and she had almost brought herself to forget about Iris Leame. Work in the P.T.S. was partly responsible for this. It suddenly got to the interesting stage. They were sent on their first taste of ward duty.

'Are we to be trusted near the patients, d'you suppose?' Sally asked, in surprise but rising excitement. So far, it had just been school all over again, but now it seemed as if she might manage to taste a little real nursing.

Cerise said gently, 'Well that won't arise really, will it? You heard what Sister Tutor said. We're to get a sight of the patients and make ourselves useful.'

'Well, how do you make yourself useful if you don't do any nursing?' Sally demanded. 'Now don't tell me we have to scrub floors and make beds?'

'Not even those things, I should imagine,' Cerise chuckled. But she was quietly excited at the prospect, too.

They were separated. Sally wasn't surprised. Of late, Sister Tutor had been regarding the two girls suspiciously, as if she was certain that Cerise was doing Sally's homework for her. But she needn't have worried. Sally's work was her own; she had discovered that she had a good memory when she could feel free to devote all her mental processes to remembering what she had been taught in class.

Cerise was sent to Women's Medical, but Sally went to Women's Accident, a big, bustling ward, bristling with frames and pulleys over the beds, plastered limbs, cages making a hump beneath the bedclothes.

She hardly had time to take a confused look round the ward when a very starchy nurse with the staff nurse's belt pounced on her and sent her to the kitchen to fetch a trolley of mugs of milk drinks, and Dinah Howard, who had come with her, was sent to help one of the ward's juniors do a blanket-bath.

Sally breathed again. Rather Dinah than herself! She was inclined to be heavy-handed with a blanket-bath, and so far she had practised only on the model they kept in P.T.S. Dinah had practised on her best friend Norma Kershaw, so she had the advantage of a live model.

Sally came back rattling her trolley, putting out a great deal of energy, and making enough noise, pushing backwards through the swing doors into the ward, to make everyone jump. The staff nurse descended on her again.

'Goodness, you're not going to be much good if that's the best you can do – look at this trolley! You've slopped all the drinks over on to it!'

In frustration, she called a junior back who was leaving the ward. 'Here, come back and mop this lot up,' she said in disgust, and took the junior's file away from her and gave it to Sally. 'This is to go down to the Almoner's office. Think you can manage it without disaster?'

Sally, rather put out by what she considered a lot of fuss over nothing, nodded, and marched off with the file.

The hospital was a big place, and after several false starts Sally found she was back at the door of the Women's Accident Ward again. This time she asked someone, and found her way down to the Almoner's office without disaster, but the Almoner wanted a file taken to Men's Medical and thought it would be a nice little job for a P.T.S. girl on her first day in the hospital. That was Sally's undoing.

The R.M.O. found her looking at a plan of the hospital on the walls of the main hall.

'Having a day off?' he asked her softly, as he passed.

She spun round, and looked up at him, scarlet to the ears. 'No, I'm on my first day on the wards and I can't find anything! It's like a maze!'

'What did you want to find?' he asked her,

pulling a funny face. 'The canteen for a nice cuppa? It might be an idea.'

She was scandalised. Surely he didn't think he was going to take a P.T.S. babe to the canteen and regale her with *tea?* 'No, sir,' she stuttered, 'I just want Men's Medical, to take *this!*'

'Then we'll go together, to keep up each other's morale, and as you don't appear to like the canteen tea, how about having some tea with me out somewhere? Say, tomorrow – no, *this* afternoon?'

'But is it allowed?' she asked blankly, hurrying to keep up with his long easy strides. 'What I mean is, I thought the P.T.S. housed the lowest form of animal life!'

'Possibly,' he allowed, with a grin, 'but ask anyone and they'll assure you that I am a law unto myself. No one tells me what to do, and when I fancy taking a P.T.S. babe to tea, why then, who's to tell me not to?'

She grinned back at him. 'You'll be sorry!' she warned him.

'You're a saucy little wench, Nurse Marston,' he told her severely. 'You have quite the wickedest grin I have ever seen … when you're feeling on top of the world. You were a very limp little tadpole the other day in bed, though. No use asking what was the real cause of all that?'

'No use at all, sir,' she said primly, as they arrived at the door of Men's Medical.

She delivered her file and went, head in air, eyes averted, so that she shouldn't have to look at him as he stood by the bed just inside the door. With determination she found her way back to her own ward without mishap, and only then did she realise that almost the whole of her hour on the ward had gone.

Furious, disappointed, she went and found the staff nurse, to ask if she could do anything on the ward.

'Oh, dear, there are loads of jobs, but to trust you with them – now dare I? Well, Number Fifteen has just slopped over herself her new bottle of orange squash and the other dimwit who came with you is making heavy weather of mopping up. Go and see how much you can add to the confusion.'

Sally refused to be discouraged at that, and went down the ward trying to remember what Cerise had said about mopping up. Not too briskly, especially if the patient has arm or abdominal injuries, but not too slowly, or the wet will sink into the blankets too quickly; don't flap, because once wet, the patient feels chilly, but appear to be quite confident of what you're doing.

Very funny, Sally thought bitterly. Cerise knows all the answers, and probably no patient would dare spill anything when she was on the ward. Sally wondered what it felt like to be helpless and to spill things over yourself, and her heart sank when she saw the frame and pulley, the suspended limbs and the general state of the bed she wanted.

Then she breathed again. That wasn't Number Fifteen. It was the next bed. Number Fifteen just had a leg under a cage, and poor Dinah – her head-girl air gone, and woe all over her – was feebly mopping up with the patient's own towel.

Sally weighed in, but it was hopeless. They would have to change the bed. They hadn't made a bed before with a live patient with a leg injury. They looked at each other in despair. Then Sally caught the malicious glance of the patient, a girl about her own age. That settled it! Bad enough for the staff nurse to tick her off, but she wasn't going to be laughed at by a mere patient!

She marched off to find the staff nurse to ask where they could find clean things for the bed, but the staff nurse was on the telephone, so Sally buttonholed a junior, who distractedly showed her the linen room and left her to select what she needed. Sally took an armful of blankets and sheets and she and Dinah remade the bed.

It wasn't a very clever job, but it was quick, and the patient was at least dry in a short time. But all the time that girl had looked at Sally so knowingly that it broke in on Sally's consciousness that it couldn't be just amusement that made the patient look like that.

She had an armful of orange squash-stained bed linen to dispose of and she stopped thinking of the patient while she searched for the sluice, the place where another junior had said, over her shoulder, that soiled linen was put. Sally found a thing that looked like a tubular steel frame with a sailcloth bag hanging inside it and dumped the bedding into it. She felt dishevelled and grubby, and very hot. She stood leaning on the frame while she took wind, and again she remembered the face of the patient: pretty in a common sort of way, but hugging knowledge that amused her, about Sally. The eyes ... they had a very familiar look, Sally thought, but not under that loose frame of flaxen hair, tied in a scarlet bow. No, where did those eyes belong?

As she fought with her memory to call back the picture she needed, Sally found herself slowly growing cold. Yes, she knew that girl all right. She had seen her before all right, and the girl had seen Sally, many times. But why, why should that girl come to this hospital? What malignant Fate should have thrown her under Sally's feet today of all days? Useless to argue that this hospital served the whole district, which included the hotel where Sally had gone to work, after Bruce Carmichael's patient had found the job for her. Useless to tell herself that as she was on the P.T.S. register as Number Five she would just naturally have been sent to this ward, because that was the pattern – Numbers Five and Six on the register went to Women's Ward Five. It was as simple as that. But did this girl have to be there, at this time?

Dinah looked in. 'Come on, we ought to be going. We have to see Sister to get permission to clear off. What's wrong?'

'Nothing,' Sally said flatly. But there was, there was. Everything was wrong. That girl, with the knowing look and the maliciously amused eyes, knew all about Sally. Had she not seen that girl, with the blonde hair neatly piled on top under a maid's cap, standing in the background, that day at the Wishing Well Hotel, when there was all that flap going on about the missing diamond necklace? And hadn't that girl been standing near when Sally had discovered the thing in her coat pocket?

CHAPTER EIGHT

Emma Grice. That was the girl's name. Sally remembered it, and her. She remembered the girl with sudden force, because that little plump blonde was a type that Sally disliked most. Not exactly cunning, but certainly not straight; not exactly anything, but all things to all men. A girl who could be your enemy much more easily than she could ever be your friend.

Sally pulled herself up smartly. Well, what if it were Emma Grice in that bed? What if she did know more than Sally found it comfortable to accept? What could the little brute do? Nothing, Sally told herself firmly. If she said anything to anyone, they would at once demand to know why she hadn't spoken up before, long before!

Sally went back to the P.T.S. feeling considerably less worried. She settled down to her books, and Cerise, coming in rather pleased with herself, looked in surprise at Sally.

'Why this passion for book work?' she asked with her small smile.

Usually Sally would retort with a 'Very funnee, I must say!' kind of repartee, but not today. Instead, she said unsmilingly, 'I've just got to get through the exams. I've just go to!'

Cerise sat down and stared morosely at the girl who had become her friend. 'Any special reason, or just a sudden realisation that time waits for no man, let alone P.T.S. infants?'

'You could say that,' Sally replied. But frankness was usually the line between them, so she burst out: 'But what is nearer to the point is that dear Dr Carmichael means what he says! This is my last chance! Goodness, haven't you noticed how he's breathing down my neck lately? When it isn't a letter, it's a phone call or a visit in person – and that business of visiting his beloved cousin, our esteemed Matron, cuts no ice with me! He's just keeping tabs on me, and if I fail, he'll pounce!'

'I agree with the feebleness of his excuse about seeing his cousin, our Matron,' Cerise murmured, thinking. 'I never did think that argument held water from the start. After all, when he does come, how long does he spend with Matron? No more than a duty ten minutes, or as long as it takes to throw back a cup of her ghastly China tea and hop it,' she went on, with unusual inelegance. 'But I would have said there was another reason why he haunted you, Marston!'

Sally's head shot up in alarm. 'You think he *knows?*' she asked unguardedly.

'Well, since *I* don't know, whatever it is to know, I can hardly say,' Cerise said, smiling faintly. 'What I would have said was, he's keen on you.'

'Oh, my hat, *really!*' Sally exploded. 'What a truly daft thing to say! Of course he isn't! I tell you, he doesn't like me at all, or why would he have got on his high horse in the first place?'

'Because he cares?' Cerise hazarded softly. 'Well, it's no use looking at me like that, Marston! You did ask me, and my considered opinion is that if I were a man and looked at a girl as he looks at you, and if I'd gone out of my way to get her into the same hospital that my own cousin was Matron in (which you must admit is stretching the family bond just a little in the sense that if you make a mess of everything, it'll be smirching Matron's record as well!) then I'd expect everyone to think I was keen on that girl!'

'Quite a speech,' Sally commented.

'Sorry,' said Cerise, 'but it interests me, now you come to mention it. I mean, you said he was a G.P.?'

'That's right.' Sally was red-faced, surly, now.

'And he has no partner?'

'No. He grandly carries on alone.'

'I wouldn't say grandly. It must be inconvenient at times, especially when you keep popping abroad to help a couple of patients,' said Cerise, staring at Sally. 'What happens to his practice while he's going to Switzerland to see your parents? A bit expensive, too, I would say.'

'He's not hard up, so he tells me,' Sally shrugged. 'Anyway, there's a sort of loose arrangement with two other local doctors, that they split his patients between them when he's away.'

'Still, he must like someone in your family to go to so much trouble. Allowing for having found a nurse for your parents – from this hospital, I think? – and found a specialist for them, and settled your mother into a place in Switzerland, and keeps popping out to see her – well, I ask you. Not normal procedure, surely? Once they've got the patient settled in with the top man, they leave it. Their own day's work to tackle, if you see what I mean.'

'So?' Sally stormed.

'So,' Cerise said quietly, looking away, 'if I were you, I would regard him as the owner of the best shoulder to weep on, when whatever happened to you today on Women's Accident becomes too unbearable to manage alone.'

Sally shot to her feet. 'Who told you anything about what happened today?'

'Dinah Howard was telling Norma Kershaw about it and I overheard and questioned her. She didn't like telling me, but I pointed out that you were my room-mate and I had as much right to hear about it as Kershaw had.'

'And what did dear Dinah say?'

'She said you looked quite ill, after helping with a patient called Grice. She thought you might know her. After you'd left the ward, Howard got sent to help change a bed further down, and when she passed Miss Grice's bed–'

'*Miss* Grice, as you so grandly call her, is a nasty little floor maid in a small hotel called the Wishing Well, if you want to know – the hotel (in case you start putting two and two together) where, in case I haven't already told you, I was employed as receptionist, and left in a hurry.'

Cerise blinked. 'Well, that girl in the bed there, Marston, is telling the patients on either side of her that a certain new nurse is the same one who was employed in the hotel where she worked, and who left in rather a hurry after there was some trouble over a customer losing a diamond necklace.' She looked hot and flushed as she said it. 'Well, I thought you ought to know. You're not likely to find out from any kindness on Dinah Howard's part.'

Sally got up and went and stood over at the window, staring down at the scene below. As always, nurses went to and fro, in twos and threes; white coats, short and long, crossed the bright green on the close-cropped turf, and today a gardener was making a pretence of hoeing one of the borders – a deceptively peaceful scene. The hospital crouched back like a benevolent old lady, a shabby yet strong pile of bricks and mortar, every window a-twinkle in the sunshine. A good place to work in, Sally thought savagely; a cut above the stables at the riding school, and certainly a cut above that small hotel where she had been so thoroughly wretched and frightened. That last day at the hotel she would have given the world for someone to confide in, but there had been no one. If it were true about the way Bruce Carmichael felt about her (which she didn't really believe) then how was it she hadn't been able to confide in him? Always there had been Roberta lurking about, Sally thought drearily.

'Isn't it *marvellous?*' she said derisively, to no one in particular. 'All I've ever wanted was to keep myself to myself. I just didn't want anyone else to come poking into my affairs. I did the adequate amount of work, so no one could accuse me of wanting to be top dog, or that I was lazy and left everything to other people. I thought if one went through life steering a nice middle course, one would be left alone!'

Cerise said wisely, 'There are people around who just can't leave other people alone, especially those who don't want to mix and mingle.'

She could also have added, but she had no intention of doing so, that Sally's golden beauty was a challenge to those less well endowed, and that Sally also had a habit of sailing smilingly through life with her chin so averted that she just didn't *see* anyone else around her. It was nothing against Sally. It was just her way. But it made so many people writhe, to be overlooked in such a manner. People like Joan Underwood (who Cerise knew was busy circulating the rumour, and dressing it up, but she wasn't going to tell Sally) and little Amanda Pimm, who was a spoilt darling and didn't like to feel that Sally overshadowed her all the time without even trying to. And that girl in the bed, whom Cerise hadn't even seen – what had she got against Sally, she wondered, to make her lie in bed and openly gossip about one of the newest nurses in the hospital, who was finding life quite difficult enough already?

'There is, too, the little matter of you attracting other girls' menfolk – well, you told me about that yourself,' Cerise said thoughtfully. 'Do you suppose this maid at the hotel thought you had done that, however unintentionally?'

Now Sally was really annoyed. 'I don't think that's worth answering,' she said coldly. 'As if I would!'

'Well, I don't know,' Cerise objected. 'This maid might have fancied her chances with one of the guests, who already had his eye on you. Well, there must have been something, for her to have made up such a story about you.'

'It wasn't made up,' Sally said, in a low

wretched voice. 'I remember now. I was standing with those diamonds in my hand, looking at them, and she was there, in a doorway. Just for a second. Then she vanished.'

Now Cerise was appalled. 'Sally, you can't mean that!' she whispered.

'Don't be a goop, Cerise!' In the heat of the moment, they had forgotten hospital tradition and abandoned the use of their surnames. 'Of course I didn't take the thing – I wouldn't know how to, and what would I want to do that for? No, I found it in my pocket, when I was putting on my coat.'

'What did you do then?' Cerise asked blankly. Her own inclination would have been to take it straight to the police, and explain. A nice uncomplicated mind that ordered her daily life and kept her out of trouble.

Sally wasn't like that. 'If you want to know, the whole place was swarming with coppers and reporters, because the old dear who had lost the thing was making such a fuss she had called the police in herself instead of just quietly telling the management about it. So I did the sensible thing. I got rid of it.'

'You – *wha-at?*'

'Yes, well, I doubt if that maid had waited to see what I did with it, so she won't know it's in the sand bucket by the broom cupboard. Very primitive hotel, that. Still use buckets of sand in case of fire. Oh, they have one or two squirters on the wall, just to show they know we're in the twentieth century, but between ourselves, I don't think anyone knows how to use them and they've probably rusted into their sockets, it's so long since they were first put there.'

'But are you mad?' Cerise gasped. 'Why didn't you take it to the management and say you found it?'

Sally came back to her and she was grinning openly now. 'They'll find it some day, if there's a fire, or someone discovers there are too many cigarette ends in the sand, for common decency, and decides to change it. You don't think even I would go confessing to such a find, with my record of trouble behind me, do you?'

And she went out, her coat slung over her shoulder, and a nonchalant air about her that made Cerise want to shake her. A minute later Sally was back again. 'I forgot – the R.M.O.'s taking me to tea. I'd better put on some mufti.'

Cerise watched her change, silent. Sally found a sweater and matching cardigan of a warm apricot shade that suited her so well that she seemed to glow. The skirt that went with them was a fine check in two shades of brown, and Sally put on, after some thought, a pair of shoes of much too smart a cut and dyed leaf green. The sort of impudent shoes that only someone like Sally Marston could wear and get away with. Sally literally danced across the room to get her plastic mac and roll it under her arm, and the grin she gave Cerise showed that Sally had already put out of her mind all worrying thoughts of the rumours and what had happened to her at the Wishing Well Hotel.

'How do you do it?' Cerise asked blankly, meaning this lightning change of mood and this radiant happiness that almost made a mantle of sunshine over Sally.

Sally misconstrued. She thought that Cerise was referring to the stirring up of the R.M.O.'s interest in her.

'Oh, that old thing! I don't know. I didn't even look at the man – he saw me first and spoke to me first.' She looked sharply at Cerise. 'How is it some nice man doesn't get interested in you? They don't know what they're missing, the clots! What ward were you on this morning?'

'A female ward,' Cerise said.

'Well, so was I, but I got sent on a message

and he caught me up in the corridor. I don't see why someone shouldn't have waylaid you on route to your ward and dated you! I suspect you deliberately look at the ground when a nice man comes in sight.'

Cerise had no answer to that, without disclosing that there was only one man in whom she had the slightest interest, and he was the one who was taking Sally out to tea.

He was waiting beside his car. It was long and rakish, like himself, and his thin creased up face broke into a pleased smile when he saw her.

'Where would you like to go in this three-hour stretch they've unwisely given you?'

She giggled. 'You choose for me, Dr Weaver.'

'Let us not be formal, then, for if there's one thing that utterly spoils a good cream bun tea, it's to be called Dr Weaver. It makes me feel ancient, for a start. Would you care to call me Jacko? My friends wished it on me, for some reason.'

'Jacko? What fun. I'm Sally.'

'I know. Of all the Sallys I've known, you're the only one who doesn't really look like your name. I should like to call you Adela or … let me think, Roberta!'

'No!' Sally stormed. 'Surely, surely I don't

look like a Roberta!'

'Only teasing. Calm down. Sally you are and Sally you'll be, you little spitfire. Now let me see, we've done twenty-five miles. We haven't got all day. What about the Wishing Well Hotel in Jopplewick?'

Sally couldn't believe it. 'It's a plot! You're getting at me, sir!'

'Oh, dear, what have I done to introduce formality so quickly? My dear girl, I happened to hear a patient on Women's Accident telling someone else that that particular place did the best teas this side of Queenswood, that's all. We'll choose somewhere else, if you don't like that one!'

'I bet she told you – she wouldn't, I suppose, be someone called Grice? I thought so,' Sally said between her teeth. 'She's a maid there. And if you listen hard enough you'll hear from her that I was also employed there once, in the reception desk. And if you don't mind, I think I'll skip tea with you today.'

'Oh, calm down. It was a natural mistake on my part. I find the best places by listening to other people talking about them. And in passing, there does just happen to be the Smugglers' Inn in Padthorpe, if you can bear to stay in my car long enough for me to drive you there.'

He looked as nettled as she was.

'How did you manage to *do* it?' she demanded, some five minutes later, five minutes of such tension in the car that he wondered it didn't shoot the roof off. 'To say I looked like the one person in the world I loathe most, I think (well almost!) and to want to take me to tea at the one hotel I earnestly want to keep away from.'

'Oh, that's me!' he said cheerfully. 'Sorry, m'dear – forget it. No harm meant.'

Padthorpe was a scattering of fishermen's houses, a few inadequate shops, a nice little grey stone church, a corrugated tin chapel, an ambitious cinema that looked frankly out of place, five big houses hiding themselves for shame behind high hedges and fruit trees, and the Smugglers' Inn. The Inn stood a little away from the rest, and it was a gem to look at, a gem to take tea in.

True, the dry rot could be smelt that hot afternoon, but the beams were really natural black, really old, and the floors weren't quite level, and Sally was enchanted by it.

'Am I forgiven?' he asked her with a funny little smiling moue.'

'Of course you are, dear Jacko, and I think in my heart you fully expected to be,' Sally said expansively. She now felt she could relax and enjoy this unexpected pleasure. 'Besides, I think you must have known about my two *bêtes noires* and just dug them out to tease me. You're a terrible tease, I think.'

'Hark at the pot calling the kettle black,' he murmured. 'I say, are you really going to tuck away all that cream stuff? Aren't you afraid of putting on weight?'

'Not me! I never put on weight. I never have to worry about my figure, which is as well, considering–'

She broke off. She had been going to say, rather unwisely, considering how many other things she had to worry about. She paid a lot of attention to sugaring her tea, and avoided his eyes.

'Sally! Where are your parents?' he asked suddenly.

'In France. Didn't I tell you?'

'Have you no relatives in England?'

She shook her head.

'I believe your half term is soon coming up. What has been arranged for you?'

'Nothing! I'd forgotten about that. Oh, I expect my dear doctor will have it all worked out – him and Roberta!' she growled.

'Oh, dear. I had no inkling of how much I was putting my big foot in it, saying you looked like a Roberta, had I? Is this doctor of yours going to marry her? Is that it? And you're casting a longing eye at him – or have I got it wrong?'

'You have!' she said quickly, indignantly.

'What a shame! I'm spoiling your cream buns, aren't I, and I didn't mean to, honestly. It's just that I did rather wonder if I could suggest something for your week-end. My grandparents sometimes like to have some of the P.T.S. girls to their place – haven't you heard it mentioned? My grandfather, needless to say, was a physician, and they do like to keep in touch. My grandmother is a sweetie. She adores young people about. Does it appeal?'

She looked helplessly at him. 'It really is awfully sweet of you, but I did rather wonder if I could go to France to see my parents. If I can persuade my wretched doctor to permit me to see them.'

He smiled ghoulishly at her. 'Carmichael, I believe he is? Matron's cousin. So you're the one he was talking about last week. No, I didn't meet him personally. Matron told me.' And he stopped smiling and looked very thoughtfully at her. 'Well, Sally, if he doesn't let you go to France, let me fix it up with my grandparents. I can promise you some fun.'

'Can my friend come too?' she asked.

'Yes, of course. Will she want to?' he asked idly. 'I thought all the present P.T.S. batch were clamouring to go home for their half term.'

Sally thought it highly likely that Cerise would adore to get away from her family, just for once, but she didn't say so.

He was a strange person, John Weaver. At one moment he seemed as young as she was, and as much in favour of fun; the next moment he was aloof from her, sitting back and studying her with amusement. She didn't know whether she liked him or not. Still, he made her break from duty that day a quite pleasant one and helped her to forget her troubles.

When she got back to the Nurses' Home and told Cerise about it, and the invitation, Cerise whitened. 'Yes, I'd heard about it,' she said, tight-lipped.

'Well, wouldn't you like to go?' Sally asked in surprise. 'Mind you, I haven't a clue where his grandparents hang out. I forgot to ask. I was thinking about something else.'

'On the other side of Padthorpe, at the mouth of the estuary. A large rambling old place with a boathouse. The R.M.O. spends a lot of his time there, messing about with boats – fishing. His grandfather, too.'

'My, you know it all!' Sally said, laughing. 'Well, at least it sounds different. It might be all right. Shall I say you'll go?'

'It depends, doesn't it, on whether your parents will be having you with them for your half term,' Cerise pointed out reasonably.

'You mean it depends on whether dear Dr Carmichael will let me go,' Sally fumed.

And of course, he didn't. With good reason, as Cerise pointed out, because Sally's mother's operation would be at that time. Bruce Carmichael said, on the telephone, quite firmly, that it wouldn't be at all the thing for Sally to be there, spending her half term. It would worry her mother. Her mother specially wanted her to have a good time in her short and precious holiday, and her father agreed. He, it seemed, was far from well, but Bruce had kept it from Sally so far. Bruce endorsed the idea of her going to the R.M.O.'s grandparents – he had heard about it from Matron.

'So, my lamb,' Sally said savagely to Cerise, when she had slammed down the telephone and returned to their shared bedroom, 'we go for a wildly exciting holiday to the R.M.O.'s grannie.'

She had no idea whether Cerise really wanted to go, even when it came to the point of the R.M.O. calling for them to personally drive them down – a thing which rarely happened, it seemed. All the other girls in their set had already departed for home. Norma Kershaw had decided not to come back – nursing bored her, she said. And Amanda Pimm had been requested to look for something else, as her work was so consistently bad that even she had had to admit that only a miracle would get her through her exam. Joan Underwood had been given a warning, but she had hinted darkly that if she could find something else to do she, too, wouldn't return.

'Not a sparkling lot, are we?' Sally said happily, sitting between John Weaver and Cerise, and recounting the story with gusto. 'Only Cerise here is any good, and that's because hundreds of people in her family are already connected with medicine.'

John Weaver glanced at Cerise with a new interest and Sally felt rather pleased with herself. When they arrived at the big white house with the flag on the flagpole on the roof, and the cobbled garden with tubs of plants, tidily leading to the boathouse, she decided she would get the grandparents interested in Cerise Oldham's family, too, and see if she could manage some match-making this week-end. The R.M.O. was getting rather too friendly with Sally herself for her own comfort.

But she didn't get round to any match-making for Cerise, as it happened. Something else happened to tip her week-end upside down and to leave her shaken and gasping.

It happened after tea, during which the old people – not so old, really, and quite modern in their way – talked solidly about the shore-line on which they lived. They didn't give Sally or Cerise a chance to mention the hospital or their own lives, because quite clearly the old people thought that this week-end had to be made completely different and the only way they knew how to make it different was to discuss the thing that interested them most: the sea. Boats on it and fish in it, and everything connected with both.

Cerise concentrated on keeping her eyes averted from John Weaver, who looked to her devastatingly attractive in trim slacks and a thick sloppy sweater with a turtle neck. He was so different from the man who had shown her, on the wards one day, how to see that a saline drip was working properly, and whose touch – when he was guiding her fumbling fingers to adjust the tube – had sent electric shocks through her and troubled her so much that her written work had been all wrong the next day.

She had even tried doing without her glasses, in the hope of looking sophisticated, or at least less unattractive, but all that had happened was that she collected some bruises through running into doors and other obstacles that she couldn't see in time.

Sally fought to tamp down her boredom. Small craft held no interest for her whatever, but she wished heartily that they could go swimming, or something – something to get her away from her kind host and hostess without seeming ill-mannered. John Weaver was no help at all. He kept looking at Cerise as if he hadn't seen her before.

And then quite suddenly reprieve came. The maid came in and said someone was on the telephone for Nurse Marston.

For no reason at all, Sally thought of her mother. It must be Dr Carmichael to report on the operation. She stumbled a little as she got to her feet, hastily telling them what she thought it was.

They were all very much concerned, and John Weaver put his hand under Sally's elbow to steady her.

She was shocked and ashamed because until now she hadn't worried at all about her mother's operation. Had not Bruce Carmichael insisted all along that it would be all right? But this telephone call had the touch of premonition about it, and all the time she was forcing herself to walk out of the room towards the instrument in the small sitting-room at the end of the hall, she was wishing she didn't have to go and answer it.

She picked up the receiver. John Weaver hovered, looking concerned. But it wasn't Bruce Carmichael, and for the moment Sally didn't recognise the voice.

'Who is it?' she repeated, sharply this time.

'You won't really know my name, even if I give it,' the voice said smoothly. 'Are you alone? Well, you'd better be, hadn't you? I shan't keep you long, but what I have to say is rather private, and they tell me my voice carries.'

She flushed, covered the receiver and turned to the R.M.O.

'It's ... not about my mother, actually,' she said apologetically, but he noticed she was deathly white. 'I'll be all right now, honestly,' she added, and waited for him to go.

'All right,' he said slowly. 'I'll be near at

hand. Call me if you want me.'

She nodded, and turned back to the telephone. 'How did you know I'd be here?' she demanded.

'A patient told me where I'd find you,' he said. 'She heard some nurses talking about you having a half term on the bounty of the R.M.O.'

'A patient?' John Weaver heard her say sharply. He didn't like this at all, nor the way she was looking, as if blind terror had taken possession of her, so he kept his door ajar and listened unashamedly.

'Yes, name of Grice. Convey anything to you? Ah, I thought it would. Now, let's not waste time, my dear. I have to see you, about a little matter I needn't mention over the telephone. Let's just say you did a neat job making something vanish, shall we? Well, I want to know where it vanished to, and then you can be a good girl and make a few more things vanish ... for me.'

CHAPTER NINE

Sally replaced the receiver, and stood there holding her head. She felt sick. First Emma Grice, and now this man, and they knew, both of them. *They knew.*

She couldn't think straight. Somehow her mind refused to function. She couldn't call to mind the man's name or what he looked like, yet she knew him. She knew him as if he had lived next door to her, yet she couldn't call his face to mind nor remember his name: she could only feel his sinister personality reaching out to her, through his voice on the telephone. And she was afraid.

She had never been afraid in her life before. Practically every other emotion possible had ripped through her slender young body at some time or other, but never fear. She didn't like it and she connected it with that man and blamed him for it. She felt that perhaps she might not fear him if she could see him, know his name. She wished she had agreed to his meeting her. She had put the telephone down without answering that one. Yet she knew inside her that it didn't matter. He would be there, at the time and place he had mentioned, and if she didn't present herself at the same time, he would come here to fetch her.

Impatiently she decided that she would rather know, go there and see him, get it over with, than live with this terrifying sick feeling, not knowing.

The R.M.O. strolled out from where he had been standing and towered over her. 'Phone call finished? You didn't say much,' he observed. 'Want to tell me about it?'

She shook her head. 'I want to apologise for it coming here, where I'm only a guest. It wasn't my wish. I didn't even know about it. I thought … it might be about my mother's operation, but it wasn't.'

He watched her lovely mouth go tight-lipped. She was very angry about something. 'What was it about?'

'That job I told you about. I left rather precipitately. One or two untidy ends he wants to clear up. I have to meet him. Would you mind if I went? It looks awfully bad, as if it can't wait until this week-end's over, but he says it can't.'

'All right. I'll drive you there. Where, by the way?'

She looked alarmed. 'Oh, no, that won't be necessary, thank you, Jacko. Just somewhere along the river. It won't take long. Please – you look after Cerise. She's very nice, really.'

'You're pathetically eager to convince me of that,' he smiled. 'I've got eyes, haven't I? All right, she's a nice girl. But it's you I'm worried about, and I really think I shall have to insist on going with you.'

'All right,' she said, suddenly capitulating. She could see he wouldn't take no for an answer. She decided to slip out when he was otherwise engaged. It was the only way.

She managed to slip out in time for her meeting, while the R.M.O. was on the telephone. The grandparents, having exhausted their fund of reminiscences for the time being, had retired to rest, leaving the two girls to their own resources. Cerise, who was fond of cats, had found one with a new litter in the stables. Sally didn't even tell Cerise where she was going.

The man on the telephone had said he would meet her at a place called Mackley's Quay. Sally didn't know where or what it was, but when she reached the river bank some boatmen told her, pointing to the jetty where a knot of men stood around looking down at a trim little white ketch.

When she arrived there, Sally found that all the men but one were local boatmen, in stained jeans and guernseys, their faces weatherbeaten, their hands gnarled. The other man stood head and shoulders above them, in an easy pose; in his way a typical product of the local yacht club, in neat white flannels and navy blazer, a silk scarf tucked in his open-necked silk shirt. He was talking easily and pleasantly, and when he saw Sally he broke away from them with a charm of manner which puzzled her. Surely this wasn't the man on the telephone?

But it was, and she knew his voice the moment he spoke, though she still couldn't remember his name.

'Oh, yes, my dear, the little girl from the reception desk at the Wishing Well. No doubt you recall having seen me before?'

'Yes, I remember you … vaguely,' she said, frowning, still striving to remember his name. 'I'm sorry, but I can't remember each individual guest, and I honestly don't see how you think you know anything about me.'

He stopped being wary. Quite obviously she was telling the truth and couldn't remember him. Equally obviously she was nettled that she couldn't remember him because of his knowledge of herself.

'Well, my dear, let's take a walk. I'll show you one or two trim craft while we talk. It will look more natural. Meantime, you and I have quite a lot to settle up. You see, though you apparently don't know me, I know quite a lot about you. Not that I don't care for what I know, mark you.'

'I suppose Emma Grice told you,' Sally said fiercely. 'Emma Grice doesn't know all of the truth!'

'I don't suppose she does,' he agreed. 'And after all, that's all to the good. We don't want that tiresome young woman hanging around our necks, do we, because you and I are going to be friends. Well, associates, shall we say?'

'Look, before we go any further, who *are* you?' Sally demanded.

'That's hardly the point,' he said, quite firmly. 'The point is that I happen to know that that diamond necklace that was "lost" was in your coat pocket.'

'Emma Grice!' Sally said fiercely. 'I found it there. I've no idea how it got there!'

'That's very likely,' he broke in smoothly. 'But that's not the point at issue. The point at issue was that you were very slick indeed at getting rid of it. That's what interests me.'

'Why? Was it yours?' she said truculently.

'Let us concentrate on the interesting slant of why you didn't go to the management with what you had found in your pocket, or even to the police. I don't believe you considered that course very sensible in view of a rather odd record you have of being on hand when something valuable gets lost. Right?'

He watched with a half smile as the red tide ran up her cheeks.

'Oh, don't be bothered about it. I've known a lot of people in my time who had that odd thing about them. I'm not saying that they were responsible for the loss of the valuables, but I am saying that very few people might be persuaded to believe that. That being the case, it's sometimes very awkward, as in your case. You had to get rid of the thing, for your own sake, and you did it pretty thoroughly. Where?'

'If I tell anyone where, it will be the police, at a date when I no longer have to worry about making a lot of fuss and publicity.'

'What date will that be?' he asked softly.

'How do I know? When some family matter is over.'

'Oh, I see. But you must understand that your family and its affairs is of no interest to me. I want you to do the same little trick with another valuable piece, for me.'

'You want me to steal? You must be out of your mind!' she stormed, and turned to leave him.

His hand shot out and held her arm; not hurtingly, but too firmly for her to break away.

'I didn't say steal, now did I? I just want you to hide it, for a joke. The sort of joke that the owner has on the insurance company when he claims for loss, and then the person playing hide and seek "finds" it again for him. It's being done all the time, my dear, but I haven't discovered many good hiding places. That's the trouble. And you have, it appears … unless you just kept it, or hocked it. But no, I don't think so. The police have been covering the pawnshops pretty thoroughly. No, you don't seem the type for that little lark. But of course you might have passed it on to someone else. I wonder?'

Sally's eyes were stormy. 'You've got it all wrong. I don't know how that necklace came to be in my pocket! I just knew it hadn't come there by accident and frankly I wasn't going to be found with it on me, so … I got rid of it.'

'Where?' he said softly, and very gently twisted her arm so that she winced.

'You're hurting me!' she said, raising her voice.

Two people appeared through the trees. It was too late to let Sally go, too much of a risk, before he had straightened things out with her. She was quite likely to rush up to them and tell them he was molesting her. So he did the next best thing. He swung her to him and put his arms round her, tight, and his mouth came down hard on hers.

The people passed – a man and his wife, exercising the dog. They went by in significant silence.

After they had gone out of sight and earshot only did he let Sally go, but he kept hold of her right arm. There was a glint of battle in her eyes and he wasn't sure what she would do to him.

'Hold your horses,' he said, in a more gentle voice. 'I had to do that! It was the only way to silence you at short notice. Listen! You don't have to work with me, you know. If you won't tell me what you did with the thing, then that's all right. But don't be surprised if the police hear a rather odd story (anonymously given over the telephone, of course!) about a girl who left the riding school rather hurriedly after she was discovered by Captain Philpotts in his study when she had no business to be there–'

'I was sent on a message!' Sally said hotly.

'Oh, come now, who on earth would believe that? Anyway, as I say, the police would only be interested in hearing that a valuable trophy vanished after that. And quite oddly a valuable diamond necklace vanished at the next place where that same girl went to work. The two things together, do you see, wouldn't really look good!'

'Why would you do that? It isn't true, but as you say, it wouldn't look good – but what have I done to you to make you pick me out for special attention, anyway? I was only in that hotel reception desk such a little while. I don't know why things began to feel awkward, unpleasant – unless someone told them how I left the riding school, but who would do that?'

She was speaking now half to herself, not looking at him at all. 'Iris Leame? But would she hate me as much as all that?'

He laughed shortly. 'Let's go, and you can think it out on the way. I'm sure you'll come to your senses.'

'Yes, but why, why? Who *are* you? What's your name? What do you really want? It isn't sense that you want me to hide things for you – that's a daft story, for a start!'

'No, my dear, not daft at all. I'm thinking about dropping a package into the hospital for you, if you will tell me where things are left, when doting families deliver by hand, not trusting to the post. This will be diamonds of a sort–'

'No! No, you mustn't do that!' she exclaimed.

'–and you can keep them hidden in one of your famous hiding-places, until we have to "find" it and return it to the owner. Simple. You'll get a cut, too. Not a very large one, it's true, but you'll get something for your trouble. If you had no record, you'd get a much larger cut for the risk you'd be taking.'

'Record? I haven't got a record!'

'Oh, haven't you? It's a dramatic word, my dear, but it really does depend on how it sounds to the authorities – don't forget, you've been a silly girl and made quite a lot of enemies.'

'But how? Why should people hate me?' she whispered, her eyes stormy, but puzzled more than afraid. 'I just want to mind my own business.'

'You went a jolly funny way about it, didn't you? I mean, for a start, poking and prying into poor old Philpotts' study–'

'I did not poke and pry!'

'Well, his wife thought you did, for a start. You must have known she was in there with a friend of hers, or why would you stick to that feeble line of the message, which really wasn't necessary, from what I hear!'

'How did you know what happened at the riding school?' Sally demanded suspiciously.

'Philpotts is putting it around for everyone to hear about,' he said blandly. 'Especially the bit about the cup. Of course, the poor lad didn't know his wife entertained her friend in his study, but everyone else in the riding school did. Then again there was the chap Iris was keen on – Farrell. That was silly of you to encourage him!'

'I did not encourage him!' Sally stormed. 'I could never get rid of him!'

'Quentin's a nice chap. I won't have you say he's ever a nuisance to a girl. Anyway, he isn't the only enemy you've made, which isn't surprising since Iris has given him hell since you left. There's Iris herself – she didn't care for you spoiling all her weekends. And little Polly Venables – I feel really sorry for her!'

'Polly who?'

'Come now, you know Polly Venables. You must do, or you wouldn't have been on such terms as to press the use of your anorak on her.'

Sally blinked. '*That* girl! Was that her name? I never even knew it. She was new, so new she forgot to bring something warm and weatherproof, the clot.'

'Well, be that as it may, she isn't out of hospital yet, and she blames you for what happened to her. Well, it stands to reason, you must have known that horse was no good or you wouldn't have schemed to get someone else to ride it in your place.'

Sally looked up at her tormentor with loathing. 'I did a kind act, *stat.* I knew nothing of the antics of that horse, and I didn't care one way or the other about that girl except that if I see someone cold and I'm not using my thick wear, I usually lend it. It makes no odds to me.'

'A very unlikely story, my dear. But it serves to assure me what a facile little liar you are, and it ought to make you realise just what the odds are against you when I tell you that all those people don't just dislike you. They actively hate you and they'll do anything they can to bring you to book. (Lovely expression that, isn't it?) But you see, since you're presumed to be no good, and connected with the other robberies (or shall we say, mislayings of valuables?) that have happened at the Wishing Well Hotel since you left, you might as well come in with me and be of some use, mightn't you?'

He was speaking very softly now, and it teased her, the memory of where she had heard those soft tones before. But she couldn't remember, so she shrugged her shoulders and walked on, her thoughts whirling round her head.

What an untenable position she had got herself into! How had she got into such a mess, and what could do to get herself out of it, before this man involved her further in his beastly little connivings?

He insisted on walking her back to the house belonging to the R.M.O.'s grandparents, and nothing she could say would stop him. She prayed no one there would notice, but of course, there looked no harm in her companion. He strolled along easily in his elegant yachting clothes, and he looked every inch a personable member of local society. Nothing to worry about so far as his outward appearance was concerned! And the local boatmen seemed to know and like him, too. But supposing he wouldn't go and she had to ask him in?

She said a very firm goodbye at the gate,

and to her surprise he went, with a mocking half bow, and no further trouble.

Cerise came downstairs at a run to meet her. 'Where did you get to? I've been most embarrassed! I've been left alone with the R.M.O.'

'Thrills!' Sally jeered, but she looked curiously up at him as he stood leaning on the banisters looking down at them.

'All right, Sally?' he called.

'All right,' she assured him, and watched him stroll off into a room on the right.

Cerise, as soon as she realised he wasn't coming down, said, 'You went off with some man! How could you? Was that polite? We were on the roof looking through a telescope and we saw you!'

'Do you know him, the man I was with?' Sally asked, serious now, and with a catch in her voice.

'No, of course I don't! Am I supposed to?' Cerise asked crossly.

Sally's spirits sank. She had been hoping that Cerise would be able to tell her who he was; it was at the back of Sally's mind that he might have been pictured in a newspaper in connection with some yachting event.

'No, don't bother. I just mentioned it.' Sally sounded tired suddenly, and her friend looked sharply at her.

'What's wrong? I've just realised – you don't look too good,' she said.

Sally laughed mirthlessly. 'What do you expect? It wasn't a man-friend, much as you're tempted to believe that. It so happened that he knew me from one of those disastrous jobs I had. I told you my awful past would catch up with me.'

'What did he want you for, then?' Cerise asked.

Sally pulled herself up sharply. Where was the sense of telling Cerise about it? Would Cerise, good friend as she was, believe Sally's story? Her companion of this evening had shown her only too plainly what an odd-sounding story it was!

'What do *you* think?' Sally retorted, and as she had half expected, Cerise decided from that remark that the man had elected to be interested in Sally, although Sally didn't care for him.

'Oh, dear, you are a honeypot, you know!' Cerise sighed. 'You'll be in trouble one of these days.'

'I'm in it now, up to the neck,' Sally muttered, but Cerise didn't catch that, because the R.M.O. was coming downstairs, calling to them about a walk before supper.

It was, on the whole, a less difficult weekend than Sally had expected. John Weaver was a good companion and set out to entertain them, and his grandparents were charming too. But the sum total of it was that while Sally got more and more worried about the future, and more and more *distraite,* John Weaver and Cerise became close friends. He discovered that Cerise really liked to talk 'shop' and also that among the people Cerise knew in the medical world through her family's ties, there were mutual friends. Sally felt curiously left out, before the time came for them to go back to the hospital.

That was the time she dreaded. One day a package would come for her, and then what was she to do?

There were so many times when she was tempted to say to Cerise something like: there was a girl I knew, who did so-and-so and a man approached her and suggested he left her with a package…

But by then it sounded too identifiable a character to be comfortable, and Sally abandoned it.

Many was the time when she felt like telephoning Bruce Carmichael to ask him what someone should do for the best in those circumstances, but she refrained because she knew without being told that Bruce Carmichael would jump to the conclusion that Sally was talking about herself – he always did. She couldn't think why, and it always irritated her. So she didn't telephone Bruce.

Nor did she approach the R.M.O. because since that week-end at the home of his grandparents, his friendship had subtly shifted from her to Cerise. Cerise went around in a daze of happiness, and curiously her written work began to suffer, while Sally's improved. Sally was glad to get into a quiet corner with her notes, if only to keep other people from asking her questions, probing, because she looked so far from her old happy self. Inadvertently she found she had a good memory, and bent her energies on soaking up meaningless lists of parts of the body, interminable lists of surgical instruments, lists of illnesses, and lists of quarantine times for children's diseases. It all stuck in her head, and she grimly went on amassing knowledge, because it kept out other and far more worrying things from her brain.

But at night, after she had gone to bed, she found she couldn't keep her mind on the things she had learnt. Without the daylight and the written notes in front of her, her memory rebelled and surrendered to the tormenting thoughts, and she found herself bedevilled by such questions as: what would I do if Frank came in that door? What would I do if confronted by Bruce Carmichael, to give an account of my conduct for his 'last chance'? Could I honestly say that I had kept out of mischief and satisfied everyone, so far as my training had gone? And how does Bruce Carmichael strike me?

This was an illuminating and yet at the same time an alarming question. Just lately, she had been aware that while Frank could, at a moment's notice, make her melt in his arms, and that if he came back at any given time she would react in the same old way, she couldn't see herself agreeing to spend the rest of her life with him. She would never be able to bring herself to put her life into his hands, even supposing he were to ask her to marry him – which seemed unlikely. Sally discovered, with a growing sense of alarm, that what she felt for Frank was something severely set apart from love; it was exciting and exhilarating and slightly dangerous and demanding, but never love.

At the same time she was conscious lately of veering towards Bruce Carmichael, being prepared to lean on him. She had told herself again and again that this was purely a reflex action, from long habit – the way one would lean on one's family doctor, whether he were young and handsome, or elderly and experienced. He was there to lean hard on – he expected it and wanted it, and that was how she was beginning to react.

But it wasn't entirely true. There seemed to be more to it than that. When she thought of Bruce Carmichael, she found herself thinking unfriendly thoughts about Roberta, coupling the two of them together, and hating Roberta for the advantage she had of being closer to Bruce Carmichael than Sally herself. It was useless to remember that he had said he wasn't likely to marry Roberta. That didn't mean a thing. Sally was sure he would, if he got half a chance. And although Sally had the uneasy feeling that Roberta thought the world of David Marston, she was quite likely to turn to Bruce, who was free, and could offer her marriage, which Roberta herself had told Sally once was the secret desire of all nurses, even the dedicated ones. 'There's something so safe and desirable about a good marriage,' Sally could almost hear Roberta saying. 'A sort of haven, to creep into, away from the buffetings and disappointments of the outside world, particularly the world of hospital.'

It had been one of those days when they had been in the kitchen together, Sally remembered, when as a defence measure she had offered to wash up and help with the eternal laundry, because she had been feeling guilty and ashamed at having lost both of her jobs and was living on the family. She had felt that in Roberta's eyes she was nothing but a lazy young good-for-nothing, putting people to a lot of trouble, and thinking the world owed her a living because she was young and pretty. Sally had smarted under it.

Remembering the scene, in the wakeful small hours, Sally recalled also that Bruce Carmichael had been in the garden at the time, standing talking to Sally's father. Roberta had glanced at his tall figure as she had said that about marriage being a safe haven, and that, Sally told herself, was why she had got the feeling that Roberta would snaffle Bruce in the end, no matter who else she might be keen on. Trust Roberta to find her own safe haven!

Sally, with determination, pushed out of her mind the thought that if one could stop quarrelling with Bruce Carmichael, he might be rather nice for a husband. Sleep wouldn't come, so she occupied herself with wondering just who, among her many acquaintances, she could confide in, about this latest patch of trouble, before that packet turned up. With a little thrill of terror she realised that the moment she took that packet from whoever delivered it, she would be, in the eyes of the law, connected with the business in such a way that she wouldn't be able to get out of it. Wild thoughts of saying that it didn't belong to her, that it just wasn't intended for her, flashed through Sally's mind. But almost at once the futility of such a course came to her.

It was all such a mess. So far as blackmail went, that man in the yachtsman's clothes had certainly got it to a fine art! It was true what he said: just an anonymous message on the telephone about what had happened to Sally in the past, worded in such a way, would be enough to make an edge of doubt and she would be requested to leave the hospital. Sally knew, without having to be told, that no girl could hope to qualify as a nurse if it were known that she had ever been suspected of the things that Sally had been suspected of. It all had such an unpleasant sound about it, the way he had put it, yet Sally, writhing in sheer fatigue and irritability, couldn't for the life of her see what else she could have done, on her own.

If her parents hadn't been ill, and not to be worried, she could have gone to them and they could have put the thing in the hands of their solicitors, she supposed. But would it have happened like that, even if her parents had been in good health, and fit to be confided in? She doubted it. They both tended to take the 'what-have-we-done-to-deserve-this' attitude. An 'it can't really be happening to us' attitude. It was a favourite question of theirs: why do you have to get in these messes, Sally? Why can't you just settle down to a job of work like any other normal girl? And that just made her feel abnormal and horrible and she felt like running out, anywhere, away from their voices and their reproachful faces.

Who, then, who? There must be someone she could tell, and ask advice! Not the R.M.O. any more – he was quite clearly interested only in Cerise, who was a nice normal sensible girl *par excellence!* Not Matron, who was a cousin of Bruce Carmichael, and would undoubtedly be on his side. Not Sister Tut or Home Sister, because they would gang up together on Matron's side.

Not anyone, Sally thought drearily, her

eyes heavy and prickly. The dawn chorus started at that instant, and she felt she would never sleep again. At that moment, however, sleep was almost on her, and her last waking thought, before sinking into a heavy slumber from which she had to be shaken to awaken, was that she would throw everything to the winds, go to the police, and then go, just anywhere, away from them all, all the people who knew her and tried to pull her back into the immediate past. Run, run…

CHAPTER TEN

Cerise was bending anxiously over her. Sally opened her eyes and said, 'What's up? Is it fire drill or something?'

'Could be, the noise you were making!' Cerise said grimly. 'Were you having a nightmare or something? You kept saying you'd got to run before he gave you the packet! What's all that in aid of?'

'Search me,' Sally muttered as she swung out of bed.

It was a grey day, raining. Slopping wet

rain that drummed on the roofs. There was a growl or two of thunder, and then the rain eased off, but the day stayed grey and dreary, sticky, humid. A depressing sort of day on which anything might happen.

Sally's head was thumping because of her bad night. Sister Tutor was taking four of them over to the hospital today to work a little longer because of staff shortages. They couldn't, she said, have too much experience of the 'feel' of the wards, and they could do extra work on their notes when they came back. Most of the P.T.S. babes were rather bitter about it. Already Dinah was grumbling at having been deceived over the job. It was, she said, little more than an unpaid 'daily help', running off one's feet and cleaning up the spillings of other people, whether it was the bedside orange squash or the milk the junior allowed to boil over in the kitchen.

This day continued as it began, and Sally was aware of a miserable sick feeling in the pit of her stomach. In the post there was a letter from her mother giving the date of the previous day as the day of her operation, which set Sally's heart thumping in a slow lurching movement that increased the sick feeling. What had happened about it? Why hadn't she heard? Couldn't someone maage to telephone from Switzerland to say whether it had gone all right or not?

And as she walked through the main hall, past the porter's desk, to the stairs to Women's Accident, where she was to be allocated that day, the porter came out of his cubbyhole and pushed a package into her hand.

She took it absently. She was thinking about that letter from her mother, and the appalling bad luck of herself being sent on to Women's Accident, of all wards – where that horrid Emma Grice would still be in bed, a cage over one leg. She didn't look at the package until she reached the stairs, and then her legs almost gave way with shock.

It was in a plain brown paper wrapping, with no name on it, but stuck to the top of the package was an envelope addressed to 'Nurse Sally Marston', which served as a direction for the package.

She thrust it down her bib and hurried up to the ward, but before she reached there, a junior called her back to go to Matron's office.

Guiltily she thought that it was because of the package, but common sense asserted itself. How could it be? Who knew about it? But a call to Matron's office was not good.

'What shall I do about Women's Accident? I'm supposed to be helping out there this morning,' she asked.

The junior looked kindly at her. 'It's all right. I've got to go up and tell them what's happened. You scoot – Matron's waiting.'

Sally wondered if other nurses felt like this when sent for by Matron, with a conscience that wasn't clear. It was worse, much worse, than ever being expelled from school. Her legs felt wobbly, and she looked white and miserable as she passed her own reflection in the glass of a cupboard door. This day, she felt, would get worse before it got better.

Matron's office, however, was empty, and then a man came in. It was Bruce Carmichael.

Following so close on her turbulent thoughts about him in the night, she felt herself flushing under his steady gaze. She couldn't meet his eyes. She looked away towards the window, and she said, without quite knowing why she should say it, 'You've got bad news, haven't you?'

She fully expected, hoped, he would deny that, and start lecturing her. The grapevine, it just had to be the grapevine, with some tale or other about her.

He said, very quietly, 'Yes, I have. Hold on

to me, Sally, while I tell you.'

She shook her head fiercely and backed away from him. She couldn't bear the thought of him touching her. He frowned as he watched her, but he said quietly enough, 'It isn't the very worst, my dear, though heaven knows, it's bad enough. I came myself to tell you. Phone calls are so inadequate, and I wanted to be with you.'

'It's Mummy, isn't it? She's dead,' Sally said, in a harsh voice so unlike her own that he looked sharply at her.

'No, my dear, but things are not good. Post-operative collapse is a thing we all dread. She wasn't strong and she was worried about your father. I knew you'd want to know about it, and I couldn't tell you that over the telephone.'

'Why didn't they phone me from Switzerland?' she asked harshly, staring at her hands.

'But I've just come from there,' he said.

She looked at him then, in some surprise.

'I flew. I wanted to be here with you,' he said again, and now she noticed how haggard he looked, as if he, too, hadn't slept for a long time. She didn't understand it at all. Such super service, for just one lot of patients.

'That isn't all, is it?' she said.

He took her by the arms, and gently pulled her to him, and she stood, rather stiffly, with her face against his chest. 'She's dying, even if she isn't dead,' she insisted.

'There is ... some hope,' he told her quietly.

She wanted to cry. She didn't know quite what the reason was – because her mother wasn't going to recover, or because it was just another blow that was happening to herself – but the tears wouldn't come, and her throat ached, and she ached inside, and she felt as heavy as lead in all her limbs, and very cold, and quite ill. She had never felt like this in her life before.

'It was my fault, in a way,' she gasped. 'Her accident, I mean. If it hadn't been for me worrying her she wouldn't have gone on that train in the first place.'

He patted her shoulder gently, as he might have soothed a child. Sally went on, 'And if she doesn't get better, what about my father?'

'She must get better, my dear, for him,' Bruce Carmichael said. Sally took it to mean that he didn't think David Marston would survive his wife. Those two were as close as that.

It struck at her. She felt peculiarly helpless, and she didn't know what to do.

He held her away from him to look at her.

'I suggest you toddle off to Home Sister and let her put you to bed. Try and get some sleep. Perhaps by the time you wake up, I shall have some more news for you. I'm flying back there, you know, to be with your mother.'

She wanted to cry out: Why, why? But it didn't seem polite, so she just nodded, and let him propel her to the door. She was too stunned to thank him for coming, but he seemed to understand. He squeezed her arm as she went.

She didn't go back to the Nurses' Home. She went instead up to Women's Accident. She wasn't aware of where she was going. It was a reflex action. Her feet took her away from silence and solitude, to a place which she knew would be bustling and noisy and where there would be no time to think.

Although the junior had delivered her message, it made little difference, because she had spoken to Staff Nurse and since then Sister had come back, shouting for hands – any pairs of hands – to help with a three-star emergency. Two coaches had collided into each other on the greasy surface of the motorway, and there were more emergencies coming in than they could cope with.

While the other juniors were helping to

make up the emergency beds, and Sister and Staff were diving behind the curtains of emergencies already in, Sally went about the routine jobs of the ward, the fetching and carrying of water jugs, the B.P. round and things the juniors had been taken off for the extra work.

Because people were urging her to work faster, faster, it became something to be grateful about. She could move quickly on her feet and transport things from bed to kitchen, kitchen to bed, without actively thinking, and the leaden feeling inside her didn't show overmuch, because everyone else looked strained and rushed at the same time.

And then Emma Grice called to her as she passed the end of the bed.

'Nurse!' she said, and she managed to get a mocking note into that one word. 'Nurse, can I have a hot bottle – my foot on that bad leg is cold.'

Sally stopped short, skidding to a halt. The package fell out of her bib with a thud as she bent forward to lift the bedclothes and feel under them. She had yet to learn that any leg that has a cage over it loses the benefit of the bed-warmth. The purpose of the cage is to keep the weight of the blankets off the leg, but a vacuum is created. Emma Grice's foot was stone cold, yet it wasn't a cold day.

Impatiently Sally straightened the bedclothes, picked up the package distractedly and was about to run off to find a hot bottle when Emma said, in a sly little voice, 'Don't you want the cold bottle? It's still in there, but it's this side.'

Sally came round the bed, slapped her package on the locker to free both her hands, and carefully raised the bedclothes because of Emma's injuries this side. She took out the bottle and skidded off down the ward with it.

'Get it from the steriliser,' the junior hissed as she passed. She, too, had hot bottles for the emergency beds.

It took Sally some time to fill her bottle. She was new to the job, and found it difficult to get the stopper screwed in really tight. When she returned to Emma with it, Emma said, 'But where is the cover?'

Sally went back, but couldn't find any hot bottle covers, but she did find a small towel which she wrapped round it, and this time she didn't even listen to Emma. She slapped the bottle into the other side of the bed and went off.

An older nurse said, 'Are you Nurse Marston? Well, don't drop your personal correspondence on the ward floor,' and she pushed a letter to Sally, with her name on it.

Sally took it, but before she had a chance to think what it was, Sister came storming down the ward, came to a halt by her, barked, 'P.T.S.? Right, just what I want for a tiresome little job I can't spare anyone else for. Come along, nurse, don't stand there staring!' and she bore Sally off to the sluice where there was a fresh pile of macs to be scrubbed.

Sally had only done macs once, and she had to concentrate to keep the slippery soapy objects from slithering on to the floor. As it was, she got thoroughly wet and soapy herself, and didn't improve the state of her apron when it came to powdering the freshly dried macs before struggling to put them up on their hooks. Before she had quite finished, someone else looked in and said, 'For goodness' sake, nurse, you should have gone back to the P.T.S. ages ago. Go on, scoot! I'll find someone else to finish here!'

She went off and Sally gratefully escaped before someone else found something for her to do.

She was just entering the Nurses' Home to change her apron when she was aware of a lighter weight behind her bib. She put her hand down and found only the letter and not the package. She made the effort to remember what had happened to it. She was too chilled and stunned from her news about her mother to have sustained another shock at losing this thing. She just stood there, staring blankly ahead of her. No, it had gone. Gone completely from her mind. She had put it down somewhere, during that morning's work on the wards, but she couldn't remember where.

Later, much later that day, when she was sitting staring at the R.M.O. giving a lecture, but not really taking in what he was saying, it came to her where she had left it. On the locker beside Emma Grice's bed.

It hit her, like a blow. It was some minutes before she could take in the full significance of it. Anyone else's bed, but not that girl's! What would she do? Sally wondered.

Now she felt ice-cold inside. Ice-cold and tight, and peculiar. Not exactly ill, but not in a comfortable state at all. Her hand shook so much that she dropped her stylo on the ground with a clatter and everyone looked at her, including the R.M.O.

He noticed how white she was, and frowned. Something came back to him, about bad news she had had earlier that day. What on earth was she doing here? She ought to have gone off sick, after the custom in the P.T.S.

He decided not to mention it. Cerise had told him that Sally was often prickly and difficult if anyone suggested that she wasn't well or in trouble. He let the point go. When his lecture was over, however, he called her back.

'I heard about your bad news,' he told her gently. 'I would have excused you from your lecture – you know that!'

'I know, and thank you, sir,' she said formally. 'I'm all right, really.'

'You looked pretty ghastly when you dropped something during my lecture,' he smiled.

'Well, I just remembered I'd forgotten to do something and I'll be in hot water again. Ah, well, that's me, isn't it? I might just as well throw in the towel, I suppose.'

'Might I ask what it is you've forgotten to do this time, or is it not to be mentioned before the R.M.O?'

She wasn't in the mood for his gentle teasing, but even she had the sense not to snap back at him that she had left a package containing some valuable stolen jewellery on a patient's locker. True it might be, but she had already sounded him out with that sort of remark, and he had mistaken it for a joke and gently warned her against that sort of leg-pull, she remembered.

So she contented herself by saying, 'I left something belonging to me on a patient's locker this morning. I'm not used to being on the wards and it was a bit hectic.'

'I know,' he said gravely. 'I admitted that lot, remember? Oh, well, I don't suppose you'll get the sack for forgetting something. How was it the patient didn't notice and give it to some other nurse to return to you?'

'Emma Grice?' Sally's eyebrows shot up to her hairline almost. 'That one would have the greatest pleasure in just not doing any such civilised action.'

'I get the point,' he murmured. 'Why don't you go on up to that ward and ask someone what happened to it? Look here, I'm going myself. I'll ask for it, if you like. You'll probably get shot, come to think of it, if you go over to the wards without permission. I'll see what I can do.'

Sally's heart sank. She thanked him and departed, but it would have been a lot better if he hadn't made such an offer. Now he would surely want to know what was inside the package, if he ever found it!

She went back to her room and sat there thinking. Cerise asked, 'What on earth's wrong, Sally? You look as if all the troubles of the world were on your shoulders! What did the R.M.O. want?'

'To tell me not to drop things in his lecture even if I had had bad news before I came in. Oh, no that isn't fair – it wasn't like that really. He was very kind actually – too kind, in fact.'

She told Cerise about the news she had had about her mother.

Cerise was quietly sympathetic. Everything about Cerise was just right, Sally reflected; not too much, not too little. She would make an awfully good wife for someone like the R.M.O. Sally told herself she hoped it would come to that in the end. Cerise deserved someone like Jacko Weaver.

She had a wild urge to tell Cerise the rest of the story, but all she could think of to say was, 'And I'm in trouble otherwise.'

Before Cerise could ask her what sort of trouble, the maid knocked on the door and said would Nurse Marston go down because the R.M.O. wanted her.

'Here comes my trouble to a head,' Sally said darkly. 'He's going to want a few explanations now!'

She left Cerise looking very troubled, and ran down the stairs. The R.M.O. was pacing up and down outside.

'Look here, you haven't been having me on, have you?' he demanded, and he didn't look very pleased.

'I don't think I quite understand, sir,' she said.

'Well, this package you say you left on the patient's locker – it seems it's her birthday and a lot of parcels were brought in. Rather a dim birthday to enjoy, with all that emergency business going on all round you! Still, there it was. She opened all her presents, and she says they were all for her, those parcels!'

Sally whitened, and held her side. 'Oh, no!' she said faintly.

'Well, is the patient having me on?' he demanded. 'Or did she think that it was a present from you? What was in the wretched package, presuming there was one, or – to give you the benefit of the doubt – that you did leave it on her locker and no one else's?'

She shot him an angry look for the suggestion that he didn't really believe her, and she tried to concentrate.

'I must have left it on her locker,' she said, half to herself, 'because the letter that was sticky-taped on the outside must have fallen off. That's right, that's how that nurse found it on the floor. She ticked me off for dropping my letters around the place, untidying her precious ward!'

'You say a letter was taped to it and it was returned to you by a nurse? Well, didn't that remind you about the package? Why didn't you go back for the package then?'

'Honestly, Dr Weaver, it was little short of murder on that ward this morning, and I'm not used to all that haring about, and I was a bit dopey – well, after hearing about my mother–'

Her face crumpled for a second, as she realised that all those hours had gone by and she had still heard no more from Bruce Carmichael about her mother's condition.

'Yes, I'm very sorry about that,' John Weaver said contritely. 'Still, why on earth you went on the ward after that sort of shock, I can't think! Didn't they tell you to go sick? You weren't fit to be trusted on the wards in that condition!'

'Yes, they told me to go sick, but I couldn't. I dare not! I didn't want to *think*. I wanted something to *do*.'

'Well, I can appreciate that. Still, look at all this new fuss you've stirred up. Seriously, is it important? I mean, what was in that package, anyway?'

She looked consideringly at him. 'Diamonds!' was on the tip of her tongue, but she pulled herself up. Don't indulge in the luxury of that sort of larking, she told herself savagely. Besides, she didn't know for sure, did she? She didn't know what was in it, because she hadn't looked.

'I don't know,' she said, with relief so strongly in her voice that he was puzzled. 'In point of fact, someone asked me to mind something, just for a while. I didn't want to, but how could one refuse? Anyway, I don't know what was in it, and as it is isn't mine, I have to get it back. I just have to! And without fuss, Dr Weaver, because now I come to think of it, I'm not sure if I was doing the right thing in not putting it in a place of safety instead of taking it with me down my bib. I just didn't think, after getting the news about my mother. I just didn't think.'

'Well, it's all very unsatisfactory. Matron will have to know, I think. You'd better put it through the usual channels, via Home Sister. Now, I suggest!'

She nodded and went into the Nurses' Home, with every intention of doing just as he had said.

But Home Sister wasn't free, and Cerise wasn't in their room, so Sally sat on the bed and thought. And it was her undoing.

She thought all round the matter and it seemed to her that Fate had suddenly caught up with her so that all that she had been striving for was rendered useless in a few hours. She had been striving to qualify, for that 'last chance' of Bruce Carmichael's issuing, but that was all no good. How could it be any good? Whichever way she looked at it now, she would have to go. If she told Home Sister it would get to Matron (and to Bruce Carmichael) and she would not be allowed to stay. Further, she would undoubtedly be in real trouble for unwittingly helping someone engaged in what Sally could only feel was just as criminal as stealing.

If she ran away? Well, she might get away for a time, but she would still have to face the music, and there would be a frightful upset to her parents, and she would still not qualify. She felt as if she was in the centre of a trap with several exits and at each exit there was something horrible awaiting her.

She could go to the police, she supposed, and tell them all about it, but would they believe her? And still the same ultimate situation: termination of her life at the hospital.

With her head aching, she faced the last eventuality – if her mother didn't recover. She faced it squarely, and realised that her father would be unlikely to last long either, and she would be left alone. Well, they wouldn't have the disgrace of all this, but she herself would still have the same things to face.

She stood up and drummed on the window ledge with her fingers. 'It's a jinx on me,' she marvelled. 'How can someone have everything pile up so quickly and so horribly, without doing anything to deserve it? Well, it isn't as if I went out of my way to do anything – I was just friends with Quentin and upset that girl, and from then on things turned really nasty.'

She thought a bit more about it, and she had to concede that her bad luck had started before then. It had, in fact, started when she had met Frank Sandford.

Frank ... her heart still turned over at the thought of him, and that seemed the worst part about the whole thing. He was no good. He let a girl down. Look at him now – the last she had heard of him this time, after a week-end of delightful times and the promise of his staying permanently in her life, and she hadn't heard another word from him! He just let a girl down, without thinking, she told herself furiously.

She was so angry with herself that she felt she was suffocating in that small room. She must get out. A walk, somewhere where she could rely on being alone, to think...

She grabbed up a coat and went out, without thinking of what she was doing. It was too late to go far, but Sally had always been headstrong, and when she was in trouble she was like a small animal with its back to the wall. She just did as she wanted, and fought to do it.

She ran down the stairs with her head ducked, so she wouldn't see anyone and have to explain where she was going. Out into the main street, with the night life of Ventonbourne all around her, she half ran, her hair flying out behind. She held on to her cap just in time to prevent it from flying off, thought better of whipping it off, and pinned it more securely as she walked. Her coat trailed on the ground, and an older nurse, passing, stared so indignantly that Sally hastily did something about it, and slowed her pace.

A car kept pace beside her. She didn't know where it had appeared from, but the driver *tooted* the horn at her.

Virtuously she took no notice, and hurried round the corner, but the car came too, and got there a bit ahead of her, giving the driver time to stop and get out.

She stopped, staring unbelieving at his tall form, and his elegant tailoring, and his rueful grin as he spread his arms wide. 'Sally, m'dear, long time no see!'

'Frank!' she gasped.

CHAPTER ELEVEN

She flew to him. After the first startled silence of recognition she just flew to him, and stood tight-pressed against him, her arms clinging to him, everything else in the world blotted out. Without rhyme or reason, he was back, waiting for her, and she accepted it without question.

Frank's voice brought her back to her senses. Surprised, a little embarrassed, just a little displeased.

'I say, old dear, d'you think you ought – in the middle of everywhere, I mean to say, and in that damned uniform?'

Only one word of all that made any sense

to her. 'Uniform'. She broke away from him with a startled exclamation, scarlet to the ears, and he tucked her in the car beside him without another word.

'Where to?' he asked perfunctorily, but of course, she neither knew nor cared. She shrugged.

'Well, let's put it this way – where were you bound for?' he said gently.

'Just anywhere, anywhere at all, to get away by myself and think.'

He started the car and it slid noiselessly away from the kerb. He chuckled as he did so. 'That sounds like old times, doesn't it? Haring away from trouble?'

'Well, you know me,' she said.

He concentrated on the driving, through the worst of the traffic, and it gave her a chance to think, but her thoughts didn't help her. They were chaotic.

He was back, and his cool little welcome did nothing to dampen her ardour. She admitted to herself that she was sick and silly over him, though she knew he was no good, but all the same, his was the one friendly hand held out to her at this moment in the darkness, and she was holding on tightly to it, and not caring. He was back, her thoughts sang, to the rhythm of the engine's purr.

Presently he swung away from the main road, and followed the road to Jopplewick. Beyond Jopplewick's manufacturing contours was a stretch of wooded country with a broad river. It got grey and sluggish where it emptied itself in the estuary, but here it was pleasant, cool, quiet. All the things that Sally needed most.

They got out of the car and stretched their legs, and without being able to help herself, she fled to the comfort of his arms again. He held her to him and kissed her, quite satisfactorily, and they walked again, in the shadow of the oaks and larches, the skinny saplings and the hoary old Scots firs. A tangled wood, that seemed to cordon them off from the rest of the world, and Sally drank in the peace of the birdsong and the sense of having someone to cling to.

And then, in a moment or two, it seemed, Frank quietly shattered that feeling, by remarking: 'I knew you were in the muck, old girl, and this time I thought I'd better not leave it to others, but come over myself and try to sort you out.'

She held away from him, frowning, trying to assure herself that she had heard aright.

'You *heard* I was ... in trouble?' she said,

finding her words carefully, putting the exact emphasis on each, to be sure she got it right.

'A little more precisely than I worded it, but yes, it amounts to the same. The thought does just occur to me that you might be having a bit of a leg-pull, but no, come to think of it, I believe the problem is genuine, because you really didn't look too happy when I pulled up the car by you. Let's walk again, and you unload on me, old dear.'

'Let's walk,' she agreed, 'but first, to clear things in my mind, tell me who told you I was in trouble.'

As she said it, the thought occurred to her that Bruce Carmichael was behind this. She didn't know how, but she was always inclined to blame him. She was never quite sure – not of his loyalty so much as the way his mind worked. The way he thought was usually a clear indication of what he considered was the Right Thing to Do. Sally viciously put capitals to the words in her mind, and told herself that what he thought was the right thing to do would strike her as being a frank breach of loyalty, a siding with the enemy on Bruce Carmichael's part.

Frank again shattered her preconceived notions by remarking, with almost casualness, 'Actually, there's no reason why I shouldn't tell you, old dear. I got the news from a chap called Bosworth – Antony Bosworth.'

'Antony Bosworth?' she echoed, swinging round to face him. Her eyes searched his, and her mind worked overtime. Suddenly it all clicked into place, with a clarity that scared her. *Antony Bosworth.* The name thundered through her mind, and she found herself saying, softly, almost under her breath: 'Yes, that's him. That's who it is. The man in the yachting clothes. The man-friend of Captain Philpotts' wife.'

'Quite, old dear, and he wasn't far wrong when he said that you'd recognised him, in spite of you putting up a thumping good show of not recognising him from Adam.'

'I wasn't putting up a show,' she said hotly. 'I didn't recognise him. I felt I knew him, but I couldn't put a name to him, and he wouldn't tell me who he was. I suppose you know, then, about his visit to the relatives of the R.M.O. when my friend and I stayed there the half term week-end?'

'Yes,' Frank said ruefully. 'That visit! He doesn't know now whether he did the right thing or the wrong, but still, we do now know that you recognised him–'

'No, I tell you! And I wouldn't have remembered his name if you hadn't said it just now! It came to me!'

Frank swore softly under his breath, but his smile flashed out again almost at once. 'Oh, well, not to worry! As I put it to the chap, if you didn't recognise him now, it would come back to you later. Girls like you worry round a thing till they get it in the end. That's one of the things I always liked about you so much, old dear – that restlessness. One can always land up with a placid girl, they're two a penny. But oh, lor', how they do bore one after a bit. Now you, old dear, you never bore a chap. Tire him out, yes, at times, but never bore him.'

'Thank you very much,' she said bitterly. 'Now I know just where we stand, don't I?'

'Oh, I don't know, love,' he said, and much against her will, he pulled her to him again, and drowned her doubts with his rain of kisses. He could kiss softly and make a person feel like floating away on a pink cloud to a land where trouble was an unknown name, and he could tear at the senses with a thunderburst of hectic kisses that demanded while they gave, and raised the blood heat to fever pitch. *Fever.* Yes, that's what she had, where Frank was concerned, she told herself frenziedly, as she strove to keep her mind clear to question him again.

She disliked and distrusted his hold over her to such a pitch that she was now disgusted with herself, and she pushed him away. 'Whose side are you on, Frank?'

'Side? Oh, you know me, old dear – I don't take sides. Nothing in it for a chap like me. No, I like people in the mass. Everyone's got something to give, even that chap Bosworth. Clever chap, that!'

They were back to that terrible year again.

'I don't understand how you met him – I just don't believe in coincidences – or was it indirectly through you that I got that awful job at the riding school?' she asked, a catch in her voice, as she tried to think back. 'No, that couldn't be! I was to meet you that day, while I was at school,' she said, thinking. 'And you didn't come, and one way and another I got so late, I was caught, out of bounds into the bargain…'

'Always been sorry about that, old dear. Heard about it from one of the gardener chappies, as you know. I never thought you'd be caught – a clever girl like you. And I do assure you, you didn't get any job through me – not that I know of.'

'But if you knew Antony Bosworth – why

didn't you tell me, anyway?'

'Oh, come off it, old dear,' he begged, in astonishment. 'Now have I ever opted to tell you the story of my life? Wouldn't be the thing, you know! Not incumbent on me to tell you anything about myself, really. But just for the fun of it, I will tell you how I met him – actually, it was through you.'

'Me?'

'That's right, old dear. No coincidence, I assure you, but a perfectly natural sequence of events. To re-cap, as they say in the best circles, I was looking for you. Not at school (as I said) so I pushed around, gently enquiring (you know, saying the wrong to get the right, sort of thing!) and couldn't make any progress at all. Then one day I saw you, riding some ghastly animal, all on your own, and looking untidy, not glamorous at all, and very, very unreceptive. Well, I toddled home and had a good think about that. Heavens above, I asked myself, what's happened to my well-groomed, soignée Sally? Then I had a brainwave.'

'Go on, I'm listening,' she muttered wrathfully.

'Why don't I, I asked myself, telephone Sally's own home–'

'Oh, *no!*'

'Yes!' he said triumphantly. 'Come clean, sort of thing. Tell the parents I was, at the moment, and depending on you for the duration, your best lad. And I did. It worked. The jolly old parents were quite intrigued to find the chap who might some day be in the family–'

'Frank, how could you? You know you never intended marriage!' Anger, and something else, was in her voice – a bated-breath sort of tone. She had flung out a feeler that might, or might not, get the answer she had wanted for long enough.

But Frank was too old a hand at the game to slide into that particular guileless trap. He neatly side-stepped it, saying, 'Well, old dear, that was how I felt at the moment, but since then (and entirely on your side, I fear!) much water under the bridge, as I discovered when they told me you were at the riding school and I went there. Boy, did you leave a trail of broken-hearted males in that quarter!'

'One, in point of fact,' she said icily, 'and that was through no fault of mine!'

'Come off it, old dear – not still arguing in that way, are you?' he said, with a slightly weary note in his voice. 'You always did come back pretty smartly with an "It wasn't me!" line. Let's be honest for once. I was told, not by one, but by several people, that there wasn't a stable hand in the place who wasn't ready to black someone's eye for you, to say nothing of the boss himself being pretty silly over you.'

'Captain Philpotts? Don't be absurd!' she snapped. 'He made it quite clear that he didn't want to see me around any more, so I left!'

'That might be your story, old dear, but in point of fact, my arrival unhappily occurred just after that. (It seems you didn't acquaint your parents with the fact that you had walked out of your job mid-week.) The story, as I got it, was that the boss found you in his office, and that a valuable trophy was missing. And he let you go, quietly and without fuss? Well, that strikes me that he felt pretty strongly about you, even if he knew you loathed his guts. What man, if he wasn't silly over one of his employees, would have let her get away with that?'

Sally's face grew hot. 'Frank, what's the matter with you? You've never been like this before. And I've just thought of something – you saw me at a later date than all this happening, yet you never said a word about it. You actually (if I remember rightly!) pretended you knew nothing about what had happened to me since you'd seen me last at my school.'

He had the grace to look ashamed for a moment. But again he brightened quickly. 'Yes, well, old dear, that was a rather awkward moment you caught me, as I remember the facts. I had to think fast, talk fast too. I hadn't been briefed that you'd taken up training as a nurse. How you get around, love! And actually I wasn't particularly wanting anyone to see me in that spot at that moment. However, no harm done. So now we have our back hair right down, what?'

It seemed to Sally that the woods had gone very still. She shivered a little, because the sun had gone down and the darkness crept in with dank smells, a little mist rising from the ground; and strange rustlings in the undergrowth had an alien sound. She said what she had to say in a rather hushed voice. 'What else did you find out about me at the riding school, so that I can at least try to correct the wrong impressions you seem to have picked up?'

He ignored that thrust about wrong impressions. 'I daresay I got the whole gen, come to think of it, but I must say I didn't think you'd go the whole hog, where cheating the insurance companies was concerned, love. However, I never was a lover of those wallahs, and I take my hat off to you for the innocence in your lovely face, while your busy little hands were doing their incredible work!'

Sally gasped. 'I must be going mad! The things that happened to me since I got kicked out of school – and you, of all people, believe a completely different set of things! To think that you, of all people, should think such bad things of me!' she finished, the hushed note leaving her voice.

'Not bad things, old dear, just interesting things!'

'But they're *not true!*' and now her voice was really raised. 'They're just *not true!*'

He stared down at her. They were standing in a clearing, and she could see the moon had come up. She had no idea of the time, and she didn't care. She could no longer cope. All she could think of was that she must clear this up now. *Now.*

'You give me your version,' Frank suggested quietly and quite unexpectedly. 'From the beginning.'

She was inclined to be impatient, but as he waited she suddenly saw the sense of it.

'All right.' She hunched her shoulders,

and began, in rather a bored voice, it was true, because she had been over and over this ground, in her mind, and selecting pieces of it to tell the R.M.O., Cerise, and Bruce Carmichael. She dealt briefly with her expulsion, her mother's suspicions and the journey that led to her accident, but when it came to the period of the riding school, she was rather more explicit.

'If you hadn't run out on me, I shouldn't have been at all interested in Quentin Farrell.'

'Who was some other lass's man,' was Frank's comment on that. 'Come now, old dear, you can't blame me for a bit of daylight robbery on your part.'

'I didn't do a thing to get him!' she said indignantly. 'He showed he wanted to be friends with me instead of her, so – I was friends. She didn't have to plan to kill me on account of it, did she?'

'You have to prove that she did,' he drawled. 'More likely wanted to scare you – the feminine version of a man's good hiding he gives to a male poacher. Only in her case it went wrong and it went wrong on her best friend. Can you blame her for being livid?'

Sally was about to snap at him for that, when she remembered something. 'Oh, yes, and her livid state produced the little plot to send me to the study to catch Antony Bosworth and the boss's wife having a petting party. Do you think that that's straight honest chastising? I think it was pretty low!'

'How do you know they were there?' he asked quickly.

'Because I could smell her perfume, and now I come to think of it, that was the soft voice, the man's voice, that I heard and couldn't place, when he came on the telephone to me. Oh, and I suppose he's roping me into his little game now, because he thinks I haven't a leg to stand on. Oh, yes, I begin to see a lot of things, since meeting you tonight, Frank darling. For instance, I suppose he was afraid I would let the boss know about him, to get myself out of the mess I was in. As if I would sink to that level! I just wanted *out* – but fast!'

'So you went straight to the hotel where he was getting on nicely with a new friend!' said Frank, his face crinkling with amusement.

'You mean he isn't all that keen on Captain Philpotts' wife?' Sally was scandalised by the casualness of some men regarding their women friends. 'Good heavens, it's bad enough to be so friendly with someone who wasn't free, but wasn't it even the real thing?'

'Don't be naïve, Sally, sweet. Of course it wasn't. He was just friends with her. There's a great big wicked world outside that girls' finishing school of yours, but don't try to tell me you didn't know about it and didn't want to get into it. Well, look at it, Sally, poppet – you're in just about as bad a position as you can be, and you're arguing about the ethics of chaps like Bosworth!'

'And you,' she said hotly. 'I suppose you're going to tell me next that he was friends with the floor maid, Emma Grice!' It was meant to be a bit of cheeky nonsense to make him cross, but the startled look in his eyes suggested that it was true.

Sally thought again. After all, Emma had been a bit above herself, and she had that sort of prettiness that might appeal to someone of Antony Bosworth's type. And Emma had the package…

She wanted time to think out this new angle, but Frank didn't give her a chance. 'The whole point is, old dear, I went to that hotel to find you, but you'd gone, and Bosworth was there. Holding up the bar. We had a couple of drinks and got talking, and decided we'd a lot in common – things like finding valuables that had been lost, and keeping them in a safe place while the downcast owners claimed insurance, then collecting the reward for finding the things. Well, old dear, the owner wouldn't want to be embarrassed about it, so he'd naturally give a big reward,' and he smiled deprecatingly down into her shocked face.

'Don't look like that at me, honey, since you've proved adept yourself at hiding something that was … er … lost!'

She took the blow of this discovery, with very little to show, but it was a stronger blow than even she realised. To think that Frank, whom she had thought no worse of than as being tremendously fickle, should actually have willingly gone into this thing with these people! Why, he was as criminal as they were, because he hadn't got Fate driving him, as she had!

He tilted her chin. 'Come on, old dear, tell old Frank where you hid the thing, and then we can all sleep tonight. Give you half my share, what do you say?'

She kept her eyes down. She sensed, rather than reasoned it out, that Frank, with his hold over her affections together with his great charm of manner, would be a much worse enemy than Antony Bosworth, and in his way, more sinister, because he hadn't allowed Sally to see, until this moment, just what sort of a man he really was.

She must go carefully, she told herself. Not for worlds would she let him know where it really was, because now she saw suddenly what she had to do, and she must have that piece of jewellery to clear herself. So she said, rather breathlessly, 'I had to hide it somewhere in a hurry, after finding it in my pocket, so I took out the drawer of the counter and popped it behind there. They searched the drawers, but they didn't think of taking them out.'

'Good grief, is this true?' he exploded. 'But Bosworth told me that the owners had stripped the place to find it!'

She was appalled. 'You mean the owners *know?*'

He was scornful. 'Don't play, Sally! You must know they took the thing in the first place and planted it. Let's think ... let's think ... which drawer would it be?'

'The third down,' she said, at random, while she grappled with this new slant. What sort of thieves' kitchen had she gone into? And who had got her the job? A patient of Bruce Carmichael! That didn't endear him to her, as she savagely went over that period again and tried to remember just what he had said about her chance in such a job.

'Come on. Got to make a phone call,' said Frank, taking her arm.

Now he was all haste, to get through the woods to where he had left his car. He would phone the Wishing Well Hotel to tell them where to find it, and they would find nothing, and then what would happen to her?

All the way in the car, Sally strove to think what she could do to get away from him. She sat by his side not answering his observations, her chin sunk into her chest, and her eyes closed. Could she fling the door open at traffic lights and escape? No, some passer-by might stop her. No, that wouldn't do. Frank had the car – he could catch her up – he meant business now, it was clear.

She sat so realistically quiet that he actually thought she had gone to sleep, and when he at last pulled up outside a post office and entered the callbox, she found she was alone, in an unlocked car, in the midst of Jopplewick High Street traffic. She was out and away before Frank had got his number.

She knew Jopplewick only slightly. Where, she asked herself, could she go, to be alone long enough to do what she had to do? All she could think of was the cinema farther down the road. She had been there once and recalled that it had settees in the upstairs corridor, outside the ladies' room. There was no one in sight. It was the last half hour of the show. Just time enough to write out, on a piece of paper in her handbag, all the facts and just where she had hidden that necklace, and to put it in the envelope she had stamped ready to write her duty letter that week to Bruce Carmichael, and to post it to the Ventonbourne police station. She paused in doubt to wonder whether a statement would be valid without being signed, and it was a great temptation to just write impersonally that a diamond necklace was in such and such a place and leave it at that – but she knew very well that if the others were caught, they would soon say that she had been the one who hid the necklace. Common sense told her it would be better to make a detailed statement, keeping nothing back. In any case, she thought drearily, what did it matter now?

What could it matter? Her life at the hospital was finished, she told herself. There would be no one she could turn to, if what Bruce Carmichael had hinted about her mother were true. She knew how long her father would last afterwards. And Bruce himself? She shivered a little as she thought again that he had been the one who had got her that job at the hotel.

Where Frank was, she didn't know. She sealed her letter and left the cinema, and found the police station. They tried to keep her there while it was read, but the desk sergeant wasn't there at that moment, and the policeman holding the fort wasn't quite sure what to do. Sally stormed out of the place, and he could hardly follow her, as for the moment he was alone.

Once outside, however, Sally didn't know what to do. She kept walking, and left the main road in case Frank drove along it, looking for her. But what to do now? Go back to the hospital at this hour? She just hadn't the nerve. But she had to go somewhere.

The longer she thought about it, the more it seemed inevitable that she must get a bus back to the hospital, so she went back to the main road. And then she saw Frank's car.

He was looking for her, and now the people were coming out of the places of entertainment, swarming towards the cafés and public houses. Now it was no easy matter to search for someone.

And the bus she wanted was ahead of him, just coming out of the bus station, nosing its way into the main road.

Frank didn't stop. He kept up his spanking pace, looking from right to left among the people on the pavements. Sally watched his car and the bus converging in a hideous fascination. It all happened so quickly, there was nothing she could do. No warning she could give. He went smack into the side of the bus, his car folding like a concertina.

The crowds charged towards it. Someone said, 'There's a nurse!' and she felt herself being pushed forward. She was still in her uniform, and it struck her as tragically funny that to laymen a person in a nursing uniform was a nurse, regardless of how much or how little training they had had. She was thrust into the area and took the full brunt of the sight in the car.

Frank was bleeding badly from a head wound. She looked away from his face, but saw his leg was badly lacerated. She couldn't leave him like that. She remembered that someone had insisted in the few weeks she had been in P.T.S. that if a leg was bleeding badly, you could stop the blood by holding the leg up. It was supposed to stop bleeding sharply like a tap being turned off. She didn't think she would hurt Frank much by doing just that. It was a rough and ready bit of First Aid and she had to do something.

She heard people saying that there was a nurse in there with the driver. She heard a policeman speaking, saw his burly figure at the side of the crazily angled car. She heard the ambulance arriving, and she was aware that she had a lot of Frank's blood all over her. She was crying, too, and she didn't know what for, and she couldn't rid herself of the feeling that this was her fault. Whatever she did, wherever she went, whatever she touched, it all went wrong. Perhaps it would be as well for the other girls in P.T.S. if she had to go away. Trouble had started, hadn't it, the first day she went on the wards, and she saw Emma Grice?

So her thoughts ran. And then they came to take Frank away.

They had difficulty in getting him out. She could feel the car shaking, but they thought of nothing but the injured driver.

At last they shifted him, but the balance of the car moved as they took his weight out of it. Sally felt sick as the whole thing turned over and something struck her on the head...

CHAPTER TWELVE

The nurse who bent over Sally's bed wore a strange uniform, with a black cross hanging on a black and gold cord round her throat. Sally frowned at it and closed her eyes.

'Where am I?' she tried to say, but it was nothing more than a croak. 'Not Princess Erlana's–'

'No, Jopplewick District Hospital,' the nurse said briskly. 'Now don't worry about a thing. You just got a whack on the head. You'll be all right.'

Sally went down in to the spinning darkness again, and when she came up it was daylight and someone was bending over her leg. He wore a white coat, but he wasn't the R.S.O. she was used to. He was very cheerful, and told her not to worry, she was young and broken bones healed quickly.

She put up a hand and found that her head was bandaged. The nurse had been being tactful, then, telling her only a bit of the truth.

'What happened to me?' she asked, but he

wouldn't tell her. He just smiled evasively, exchanged a look with the nurse who was helping him, and was about to go away, but Sally stopped him with the question: 'What happened to Frank Sandford, the driver of the car?'

That did delay them. They both came back.

'What was he to you? Related?' the doctor asked.

She shook her head. 'Did he – is he going to recover?'

'It's in the balance,' the doctor said at last, and didn't look very happy. 'We'll see.'

In the balance. That reminded Sally of her mother.

'What day is it? I must know – I have to know about my mother! She'd been operated on–'

That caused another minor flutter, which ended with the needle being stuck in her arm. Sending me off again, Sally told herself bitterly, before I ask any more awkward questions.

She got it firmly fixed in her mind, then, that Frank was dead, her mother was dead, and that no one was likely to tell her a thing. She felt she didn't want to live.

The silence of her little room pressed in on her. It wasn't a room in the private wing. It was a cubicle among many glass cubicles, for unlike the Princess Erlana's, Jopplewick District was a very modern, new hospital. There were all kinds of new and brash shining things about it. No comfortable old oxygen cylinders – the oxygen was turned on from a pipe behind the bed. No comfortable hot water bottles, with the excitement of a possible leak: this place had electric blankets, sponge foam beds; there were even flush doors and curved joins between wall and floor, to prevent dust-traps. The brash newness made Sally nostalgic for Princess Erlana's, and when the she came to and saw the old familiar uniform, she almost cried. For a moment she thought she was back in her own hospital, until she saw she was still among the glass and chromium, and that the uniform was on the neat person of Cerise.

Cerise looked as if she had been crying. 'What happened to you?' she gasped. 'We didn't know where you were, and there was an awful flap on, and the police came and wanted you, but not to worry. It's all straightened out now.'

'How is it straightened out?' Sally asked feverishly.

'Well, I happen to know because they questioned me, and you'd only told me parts of it, but it seemed to fit in. The things that have been happening to you! I don't know how you manage to get into such messes!' and Cerise sounded almost admiring.

'What happened?'

'It seems that the owners of the hotel where you worked were working a racket stealing customers' valuables and making it seem as if they'd lost them, and they planted some on you–'

'Yes, I know that, but were they found? I put them in a sand bucket, and smoothed the sand over, and emptied an ash-tray into it, to make it look natural. Did they find it there?'

'Yes, they found it,' said Cerise. 'And a man called Antony Bosworth has been charged, as well. You'll have to go to give evidence, but your friend Dr Carmichael is to go with you, so it'll be all right. Isn't he nice? You never told me how nice he was!'

'Oh, so he's talked you round too, has he?' Sally said sourly. 'He won't want to go with me to give evidence. He isn't on my side – he got me the wretched job in the first place.'

'I know. He was livid about that, but it wasn't his fault that things turned out that way,' said Cerise, smiling at the memory.

'When did he tell you all this?' Sally demanded suspiciously.

Cerise looked all flustered and, Sally noticed, quite pretty. 'Oh, I've got so much to tell you, Marston, and I'm doing it all the wrong way. I haven't even asked you how you are yet!'

'In pain, of course,' Sally said grimly. 'And they've only just condescended to tell me what my injuries were. Go on, about Dr Carmichael – when did you hear all this from him.'

'Well, actually, the R.M.O. and I–'

As she broke off, Sally broke in with a little squeal of delight. 'You're not *engaged,* are you?'

'Wait till I tell you, Marston! Actually, yes, it was to be a very quiet affair, only Matron somehow caught on, and she invited us over for sherry and to drink our health, and it was while we were there that your Dr Carmichael came. Don't ask me why he came, because it was supposed to be a surprise for you. Anyway, it was while he was there–'

'Just a minute,' Sally broke in. 'When was this? How was it I didn't know?'

'It was the night you went off so suddenly, Marston. John came over after you'd gone, and we went for a walk and he proposed. It was very sudden. Well, while we were out, he was paged, and that nosy porter put it around that he was out with me and we'd looked all silly (which wasn't true!) but he must have said something to Matron before that, because she guessed and asked us to step over when we came back. Well, we did, and then we couldn't find you, for Dr Carmichael, and we were all sitting talking while we were waiting for you to come back – Sally, what's the matter? You look terrible!'

'My mother,' Sally said flatly. 'He hasn't said anything, so it must have–'

'Oh, now I'll have to tell you and he did want to be the first to say it to you. It's *all right.* He told us so.'

'Well, why didn't he come and say so himself?' Sally fumed. 'He pretends to be my friend, but I bet he was so anxious to get back to that Roberta–'

Cerise regarded Sally thoughtfully. Sally was in her most mulish mood, but she sounded near tears. *She likes him,* Cerise thought. She doesn't hate Dr Carmichael as much as she'd have me believe.

'He had to go back to Switzerland at once. Your mother is going to be all right, but she's still very ill. Poor man, he was in such a state when we had the news of your accident. He had his plane to catch and he didn't know what to do – go, or stay and see how you were. Sally, you can't say a man isn't your friend if he goes to the trouble and expense of flying here to tell you your mother wasn't doing well, and then to come back again to tell you the minute there was better news.'

'Well, where is he now?' Sally asked wildly.

'He's here,' a voice said at the door, and Cerise got to her feet.

She hastened out, and Bruce Carmichael came over and stood by Sally's side.

She stared resentfully up at him and noted how much older he looked; haggard almost, very tired, and without that superb confidence she had always privately termed bombast.

'Sally, my dear, how are you?' he asked brokenly.

'I feel ghastly. But never mind me – how is my mother?'

'There's a great improvement. I came over specially to tell you that day. My dear, what happened to you? How did you come to be in that accident?'

'As if you didn't know. It's all in that statement I sent to the police,' said Sally, turning aside, and putting her hand to her mouth, pressing the knuckles flat against her trembling lips.

Bruce Carmichael sat watching her. Absently he had taken one of her hands in his and was holding it tightly, but she didn't seem to notice.

'Yes, I heard about that. Who didn't? I'm afraid you're going to have to face a barrage of questions now you're able to talk. But I don't remember hearing about that particular man, in that story of yours. You mentioned a lot of others – Bosworth, a man named Farrell, Captain Philpotts and the hotel owner–'

Sally thought, with shock, I didn't mention Frank at all!

'But the R.S.O. here said you mentioned to him someone named Frank Sandford. Would that be the man?' Bruce Carmichael persisted.

'What if it was?' she countered. For no particular reason she felt defensive about Frank. 'Did he die?' she forced herself to say.

She didn't know what she expected to hear, but she was aware that she was all screwed up inside, terrified of what he would say. There was a future of facing Frank, now an enemy, if he lived. Frank, a man who could extract from her all the sweetness of her first love, had now turned out to be so different from anything she had expected; a man she wouldn't have looked at twice if she had known from the first. It sapped her confidence, made her feel inferior to think she had cared for him at all.

Bruce Carmichael said, 'I don't know what the chap means to you, my dear, but it isn't any use keeping the truth from you. They … did all they could for him.'

She shot her head round to look at him, to assess what that meant. Her eyes were drowned with tears, her face wet, her lips trembling.

'He wouldn't have been in very good shape if they could have saved him, and he would have had to face an ugly charge. That sort of swindle carries a heavy penalty.'

The past tense. Frank hadn't survived. Sally took it between the eyes, and broke down. But she wasn't crying so much for Frank as for herself, and what had happened to her in the painful process of learning the hard way how to give one's heart in the wrong place.

Bruce Carmichael got to his feet. So there had been another man, after all! Her mother had insisted on that all along, and she hadn't been far wrong.

'I'll let you know the minute there's any

other good news about your mother, my dear,' he said, and quietly left her. When she stopped crying, she turned to where he had been, and she was staggered to find his chair empty.

She hadn't asked him what was going to become of her. She hadn't told him how much she had learned to cherish that 'last chance' he had given her, and it struck her now that if he could go off like that, then he didn't really care about her, or what she did with her life.

She asked later for some books to study, and she settled down to work, once the police questionings were over. She was very much behind the others, but Cerise helped her. The mid-term exam hadn't been too bad, but she had a long pull to even scrape through the P.T.S. exam that would determine whether she were fit or not to become a nurse.

'I shall walk with a limp for some time,' she wrote to her mother, 'but the R.S.O. says the special exercises will do wonders. I shall do them,' she finished grimly.

Her parents were both making strides back to health, and had been told the whole story. 'It wouldn't have been sense not to tell them,' Roberta had written, 'since they were reading all the English newspapers they could get hold of.'

Roberta was writing now, in place of Bruce Carmichael – that had been so ever since he had come to see her in hospital that day.

'I wish she wouldn't write!' Sally fumed. 'Doesn't she realise I don't want to hear from her?'

'Why not?' Cerise, eternally flushed with her new happiness, asked mildly.

'Because I don't want it pushed down my throat that she's got Bruce Carmichael, if you want to know!' Sally said shortly. 'Every line she writes is triumphant. Even my mother had to rub it in by telling me it was as well she got better because she was going to lose her beloved nurse in matrimony. Trust Mummy not to realise how I'd hate to hear that!'

'What's that got to do with your nice doctor?'

Sally pretended not to hear, for despite her assertion that she didn't want Roberta to write, she apparently found the letters interesting enough to plough through to the end.

'We were all intrigued to hear how the tables were turned on that floor maid, Emma Grice, when you left the packet of stones on her locker. We think you couldn't have known that the man Bosworth had gone off her and she kept the stones to hold over him!'

Sally scowled. 'What's she talking about? I didn't even know that Emma Grice *had* been thrown over by Antony Bosworth!' she muttered, and Cerise had to tactfully tell her about that, which didn't help, as Roberta seemed better informed about something right in the hospital than Sally herself was.

'Well, why shouldn't she be?' Cerise reasoned. 'I wonder she didn't know a great deal more about it, come to think of it, only I suppose, man-like, he didn't know what was going on under his very nose.'

'Who? Who are you talking about?' Sally asked suspiciously.

'Didn't you really know, Marston?' said Cerise, trying not to laugh. 'Oh, it's too bad to tease you like this, but honestly, you can't really believe that your mother's nurse is going to marry that nice Dr Carmichael! She's in love with someone else, just as he told you. I remember distinctly you told me he said so!'

'All right, then, so she's in love with someone else,' Sally muttered, remembering that she had thought Roberta was getting too keen on her own father. 'Who is it, Miss

Clever, if you really know?'

'Actually we all heard, while you were in Jopplewick District,' Cerise said, apologetically, 'or else we wouldn't have known. She's going to marry our R.S.O.'

'Oh, *no!*' Sally exploded.

'Oh, yes,' Cerise sighed. 'I wish her joy of him. He means well, poor man, but he's a bit too hearty for me! But you can imagine, can't you, how that all began, since she was a nurse here not so long ago! That puts your mind at rest about your nice Dr Carmichael, doesn't it? He really is terribly in love with you, Marston!'

'Oh, yes, and that's why he got up and left me in mid-sentence when I was in bed, and I haven't seen or heard from him since.'

'Do I know what that's all about?' Cerise asked cautiously.

Sally started to tell her, then decided not to. Not for worlds would she admit, even to her best friend, how she had taken the news of the death of Frank Sandford.

Cerise and Sally talked very little after that. Every spare minute was spent on work. Cerise did overtime on Sally, and bent all her energies to get her through her P.T.S. exam. When it was over, Cerise was to marry the R.M.O. and after that, they were flying to

Switzerland for their honeymoon and Sally, en route to stay with her parents who were now recuperating there, was to travel with Cerise and John.

But at the last moment, this plan was cancelled and Cerise told Sally that they were going to New York instead, and Sally would have to travel alone.

Sally swallowed her disappointment. 'Well, I expect it will work out all right. If I fall flat on my face in front of everyone as I go up the gangway into the plane, it will be your fault.'

'Go on, you're so cock-a-hoop at passing your P.T.S. exam so well that you'll surprise yourself,' Cerise said rallyingly.

Sally looked worried. 'Yes, I know I passed it well, but what's it all in aid of? I can't go on being a nurse with this leg – at least, not for ages and ages. I'll have forgotten all the P.T.S. stuff when I come back to finish my training, and to be honest, I don't think I can go through all that again. Besides, you won't be there.'

'You'll be all right, I promise you,' Cerise said firmly, as if she knew for sure.

Their wedding was a mixed pleasure for Sally. She was glad for Cerise's happiness, but it made a queer lonely ache come inside her. It wasn't that she was missing Frank. She was glad to be able to put him to the back of her mind. It had been a bitter sweetness, after all. But now she was left with nothing, only the memory of how nice it might have been. She turned, with determination, to considering the journey alone on the plane.

Everything had been arranged for her, and it was still too early in the year for the plane to be crowded. All the same, it was an ordeal. She managed well enough by keeping on the ground floor of the airport, but owning to her slow progress on foot, she was last out to the airport bus to take her to the waiting plane, and it seemed to her that she was holding everyone up as she hobbled up the gangway. As she had anticipated, her bad leg gave way and buckled under her, just as she got to the top.

The stewardess came forward to help her, but a man just behind her got there first, and strong arms steadied her until she could regain her balance. He half led, half carried her into the plane, then shot back to collect his hand baggage which he had dropped.

The stewardess led her to her seat, the nearest to the door, and Sally found thankfully that it was behind everyone else. And then the man who had helped her appeared.

'You?' she gasped, as Bruce Carmichael stood there for a second, then, to get out of the way of the other passengers, dropped into the seat beside her.

'You didn't think you'd really have to travel alone, did you?' he asked huskily.

'I didn't think you'd be the one to go with me,' she choked. 'After the way you left me, that last time.'

'Last time?' He smiled twistedly. 'I seem to remember you bawling when you heard someone hadn't survived an accident, and I thought he was the one who came first with you, but your good friend Cerise assures me that the unfortunate Frank Sandford wasn't *the* one after all. Is it true, Sally?'

'I thought he was, just at first, but he let me down once too often. I think I was crying because I'd been so afraid of meeting him again, and when I realised he was no longer there, the relief was too much. I was a sort of prisoner of his.'

She looked as if she was going to dissolve into tears again, so Bruce said, 'I haven't congratulated you on passing your exam, Sally. I feel rather awful about it, considering the way I talked to you when you first went there. Those threats about it being your "last chance".'

She smiled, a rather wobbly effort. 'I think I could take anything from you, after that. I can't tell you how grateful I am that you're not letting me travel alone. It's so good of you, Dr Carmichael.'

They had taken away the gangway, and the stewardess was requesting the passengers to fasten their seat belts. Outside Sally's window, the airport bus was departing and she felt wobbly inside. This was another chapter beginning.

Bruce leaned over her to fasten her seat belt for her, as she made no attempt to do it herself.

'Do you have to be so formal? Say "Bruce" – and I'm not sure I want gratitude from you.'

'What do you want, then ... Bruce?' she asked uncertainly.

'You could, if you tried, look a bit pleased to see me sometimes, couldn't you? It hasn't been easy, getting close to a prickly little iceberg like you! I would like to have the right to look after you all the time, not just this journey.'

Her voice was as husky as his, as she said, 'Never to have to travel alone again, Bruce?'

'That's right, Sally. Never to have to travel alone, either of us. Ever again, my dearest!'

They had taken off, but neither Bruce nor Sally realised that the ground had slid away from them, and that white puff clouds were all that was in view, after the bright green of the grass of the airport. Neither Bruce nor Sally were aware, either, that the words 'Fasten your seat belts, please' were no longer to be seen because the light had gone out behind them and other passengers had already unfastened theirs. Bruce and Sally were locked in a tight embrace. Only the stewardess saw them as she passed through, and later the barman, with his little round tray of drinks, but neither of them batted an eyelid. It wouldn't be the first time that a couple in that secluded back seat hadn't paid any attention to take-off.

The publishers hope that this book has given you enjoyable reading. Large Print Books are especially designed to be as easy to see and hold as possible. If you wish a complete list of our books please ask at your local library or write directly to:

Dales Large Print Books
Magna House, Long Preston,
Skipton, North Yorkshire.
BD23 4ND

This Large Print Book, for people
who cannot read normal print,
is published under the auspices of

THE ULVERSCROFT FOUNDATION

... we hope you have enjoyed this book.
Please think for a moment about those
who have worse eyesight than you ...
and are unable to even read or enjoy
Large Print without great difficulty.

You can help them by sending a
donation, large or small, to:

**The Ulverscroft Foundation,
1, The Green, Bradgate Road,
Anstey, Leicestershire, LE7 7FU,
England.**
or request a copy of our brochure for
more details.

The Foundation will use all donations
to assist those people who are visually
impaired and need special attention
with medical research, diagnosis
and treatment.

Thank you very much for your help.